THE NEW BIZAR

PRESENTS

TETRAMINION

R.A. Roth

Eraserhead Press
Portland, OR

ERASERHEAD PRESS
P.O. BOX 10065
PORTLAND, OR 97296

WWW.ERASERHEADPRESS.COM

ISBN: 978-1-62105-235-7

Printed in the USA.

For my Mother, thank you for everything, and JR, lifelong friend and patient peregrine, and for the Chronically Awesome Jules whose feedback rescued Tetraminion from the dust and monsters.

Foreword by Kevin L. Donihe

You now hold in your hands a book from the 2016 New Bizarro Author Series. In this case, it's Tetraminion by R.A. Roth, the first NBAS release I've accepted since 2014.

It seems Mr. Roth had been sitting on this novel for three years. All that time, he wondered who might take a chance on such a strange manuscript. Then he happened upon Eraserhead Press on his Twitter feed, and the ball started to roll from there.

I mention this because it is very reminiscent of my story. Back in 1999, I was searching the Internet for guidelines. A link for Eraserhead Press came up, and I clicked it. At that moment, I realized I had found a publisher interested in the strange and idiosyncratic stuff I wanted to write, but for which there was previously no market. This points to one of the reasons I am grateful for Eraserhead Press. It gives unique writers the opportunity to have their off-kilter voices heard.

That being said, it's now time to enter Tetraminion, a dark and surreal world in which you might very well get lost. Though the madness is inescapable, I believe you will find enough connections to the real world to keep you wondering if you are, in fact, looking at things-as-we-know-them through a funhouse mirror.

R.A. Roth is one of four authors handpicked this year to give you a glimpse of the genre's future and to introduce you to new writers in the Bizarro community. If you like this book, please lend the author your support with a review, a post on social media, or just by telling a friend.

1.

McRe Wannabe

Delivered from his cocoon of isolation, Bill plunges into the sultry mouth of night, ever vigilant and on the eye for golden arches and smears of red, purple and green—markers indicating refueling stations where Bill can load up on the surplus calories required of his McRecycling habit.

The last siphoning made Bill too sore to move, but the need to replenish his depleted fat stores draws him achingly down the street like hamburger grease wicking up a paper napkin. Physical process with no emotional context. Hours of scouring the streets for an easy mark or a trick to turn leads Bill to the alleyway behind the Burger Palace. The neighborhood smells of deep fried ambrosia and exhaust fumes. Keeping to the alleyway, Bill haps on a young, slender McRe wannabe foraging through a rare unlocked dumpster for a wrapper to suck. Tough luck for the kid, but this territory has been picked clean by Bill, Pete and Pete's on and off squeeze, Helga, whose hips hold the most delicious and powerful adipose tissue in the Western Hemisphere, one hit shit, the stuff of legends.

The round smooth patch of oxidized blood on the forager's shirt alerted Bill that the kid's a McReing amateur. Classic rube miscalculation. He went for the deep visceral fat, which not only doesn't get you off, it tastes like bitter lung oysters. Lamentable that they don't they teach anything of value in school. "Dig too deep, kid, and you'll bleed out like a stuck pig. Long pork on the kill floor. Easy pickings for the vultures. And in this town, the vultures rule."

"I'll keep it in mind." The amateur runs his hand along

the inside of the dumpster, licks black rancid grease from tapering fingers. His eyes dart to a telltale mole of dried out hamburger meat on Bill's chin, a remnant from a bender with some Gold Coast brats out on a lark. Bill gave them the full downtown hospitality treatment, a suck of his good stuff and a lead sap to the skull. They woke up a few dollars lighter and a little bit wiser. Everybody wins. "I think you've had yours already, daddy-o. This is mine, see. Get lost before I hafta get mean."

"It's not a good idea to eat the black goo, kid." Bill lights up a McRe special, tobacco wrapped in bacon paper. Two puffs and it falls apart in an explosion of sparks. Rooked again by shoddy workmanship. "I've seen it turn men into monsters. The tongue swells up to the size of a football. The eyes fill with blood. Maggots pour from the ears. It's an ugly sight."

"I'll take my chances." The amateur digs to the bottom and scoops up a large congealed patty of black goo, mashes it into his mouth and begins to gag and vomit profusely before passing out.

The presence of three shadows hunched on the fire escape sets Bill's teeth on edge. It's too soon for the vultures to arrive naturally. They must've pegged the kid for a short timer and set up a watch. Vultures are ruthless and resourceful, if nothing else.

"Not today, scavengers." Bill drapes the kid over his left shoulder, about as rigorous a chore as picking up a bag of wet feathers or bundle of twigs. Maybe work as a hunger artist is more up the kid's alley. The vultures track Bill's movements in the slow motion pace of sand eroding into the sea, probing for a sign of weakness, an inroad to assaulting him without the repercussions of a fight. Vultures don't pick fights. They are janitors who clean up the aftermath. Custodians of broken dreams.

Wind-blown music and the torrid squabbles of lovers accompany Bill as he hikes his burden over to a defunct bakery on the outskirts of Germantown. Pete and Helga have been staging a squatters' protest there for over a month now. It's kind of a performance piece. Man versus society. Yeast and shattered expectations are the prevalent odors. The walls are riddled with rat warrens. The rustling gets so loud it wakes Pete up ten times a night. But Pete doesn't sleep that well anyway.

As Bill rounds the corner of the bakery, Helga appears in a window display soapy with the sketchy profile of a two-for-one sale on bear claws, cinnamon buns and some other illegible sweet treat. She stares over broken pieces of cinnamon bun, her eyes empty and intense as a mannequin's. Tied loosely at the waist, her aquamarine terrycloth bathrobe reveals a sumptuous belly button deep enough to bath in. The flecks of curdled spume on Helga's lips betray that she's been raiding nature's larder, getting off on her own supply. Wouldn't you?

"Who's the load?" Helga cocks her delicious hips, now a little lighter than before.

"Don't know. He tried the black goo. It didn't agree with him."

Helga backs away from the window. "Get that maggot head away from here!" she yells in terror from the orangey darkness. Helga's got a right to be nervous. A goo head attacked her outside a deli on Central. Big fella. Six four, three hundred pounds. The big ones think they can tolerate the black goo better than little guys. Delusional macho bullshit. The black goo targets the brain. Brain's got no nerve endings, so you don't even feel it eating you. Most goo heads are lucid right up until the second before the black goo takes control. But once they cross over, there's no going back.

"He's not that far gone," an appeal to reason Bill knows

won't work, but what the hell, he might as well try. "A glass of water and a few crackers will straighten him out." Bill repositions his unconsciousness load, and the kid croaks out a pitiful raspy moan. "Where's Pete?"

"Out," she yips at Bill with clipped finality.

"Out where?"

"Out on business." The shuffles of slippered feet trail to the door after which the snick of metal grating on metal tells Bill he's reached the end of the line. "I'll tell him you came by."

"Thanks," Bill waves at the vacant window display. "Thanks for everything."

After legging the five blocks to the county hospital emergency room, Bill props the kid in a gray chair made of hard government plastic. The waiting room is crowded and loud with a muted kind of panic. Help is on the way, don't worry. Just relax as you piss your pants with fear. A Hispanic woman with a hand wrapped in a bloody beach towel watches Bill as he paves the long admission's form with imaginary information and gibberish. The staff couldn't care less what you put on the forms so long as every blank is filled in. But if one blank remains unfilled, the staff will harvest your viable organs and sell the scraps of meat and bone to a dog food factory in China, and call the entire affair a clerical error. He tells this to the Hispanic woman, who shrugs her lack of comprehension and holds up the bloody towel as if that explains it all.

Bill lays the finished paperwork in the kid's lap and separates from the numbing plastic. A million needles and pins stab his ass in patternless waves. *I wonder what's under that towel,* he thinks and limps out into the world of the barely living.

A private ambulance roars by the county hospital as if it were a mirage.

2.
Safari in the Urban Jungle

At night, Ogilvie Station becomes a haven for closet cases looking for a cheap thrill, and Bill is as cheap as it gets. Straights tend to get sore at random homosexual propositions, so the trick to turning one of the same is to make eye contact in a way that suggests something yet suggests nothing. An hour of nebulous glancing passes before Bill hooks a three-piece suit. Standard bathroom tug. Five minutes of work for a sawbuck. Not bad. "Thanks," the man, a combine salesman from Joliet, stuffs a twenty in Bill's shirt pocket. "Thanks for everything." Never can tell who'll be a big tipper. Or maybe he was too shy to ask for change back on an illicit homosexual encounter. After the salesman leaves the stall, Bill pulls down his pants and shorts in one yank and sits down on the toilet just as a black clammy torrent sloshes out of his asshole, a violent deluge of subhuman shit that sticks to everything like tar.

Somebody swings open the bathroom door. Bill hears the Lord's name taken in vain several times before it closes. Coward. Bill, sitting at ground-zero, the fumes searing his eyes like mustard gas, isn't complaining. Besides, he's smelled worse. Maybe he should see a doctor. Not to consult about his health, but to see if the doctor might want to study ungodly crap or pass it onto his alma mater's Department of Crapology. Every university has one. They just don't advertise it in the brochure.

Bill wipes until he can't see the sense in wiping anymore and pulls up his pants, buttons and zips up and flees the bathroom to drop some of his hand-job money at the food court. Not much to choose from at the witching hour. Thai food served on wooden skewers, ice cream in plastic bowls and chicken in a paper bucket. Bill decides to stick to basics and orders a bucket of chicken with all the fixings, biscuits, creamy coleslaw, mashed potatoes and gravy. He steals away to a remote table away from the prying glances and vile looks of pity picking at the corners of his person. Poor man eating by himself, eating excessively at that. If Bill were an optimist, he'd take this reticent criticism as a call for normality, that he should eat with someone or eat less in one sitting. But as a realist, he knows what upsets the pity-priers more than anything is that people like Bill interfere with their perfect little well-adjusted world of meticulous obedience. Each time reality seeps into their field of vision, the passively pasteurized world they believe to exist curdles a little more. It doesn't matter, though. In the end, noses pinched, they'll gobble the sour blobs of spoiled illusions to avoid the bitter taste of the alternative.

Halfway through his meal, Bill sees two lawmen weaving through the tables. Rauch and O'Reilly. Couple of old time flatfoots. Corrupt as a ruptured appendix and just as deadly. They can't bust Bill for nothing they didn't see. But they can bust his chops. "Hey, Bill, long time, no see," says Rauch. His drooped eye probes Bill nimbly as a roach crawling along a baseboard. "We got a tip that you dropped off a goo head at county. You know fleeing the scene of a crime is illegal."

Say nothing. Keep eating. To mask his internalized dialogue of fear, Bill squares his gaze to Rauch and his wilted eye, the half-dead bulb beneath staring through him like he's a penny with a hole punched through it. Depression era kids used to hammer holes through pennies and thread a piece of string through the grommet. It was the only jewelry they could afford. Cost: one penny. Sometimes they'd lay a penny on the tracks for a freight train to flatten then smash a hole in the copper pancake. That's what Rauch wants to do to Bill. Put him on the tracks to flatten him smooth then wear him as a souvenir of his toughness.

"Kid's dead, Bill," says O'Reilly. He snaps up the lapels of his overcoat, alluding to a frilled lizard spitting poison and death. "Goo overdose."

"I told him not to touch it, but he didn't listen to me." Bill opens the warm waxy paper in which the biscuits are nestled safe as baby birds. *Eat me!* they chirp. In time, my children. In time. "But what can you do? The invincibility of youth makes kids unresponsive to wisdom conferred by their elders. It's the old paradox of advice falling on deaf ears, one canceling the other." Bill takes a healthy bite of a biscuit. A death chirp rents the air as the buttery layers melt in his mouth. "Kids have minds of their own. You two should know that by now."

"So you didn't turn the kid on?" O'Reilly says, dabbling in the conjured incriminations of a flatfoot on a fishing expedition.

"What, me? I hate the black goo as much as the next citizen. Scourge of the city. There ought to be a law against it."

Rauch snatches up a big juicy breast Bill was saving for dessert and takes a gigantic, wolfish bite. His dental plan fangs burrow down into the flesh as he slavers and snarls with pure animal fury, swallowing half-chewed hunks of chicken and crust. Rauch drops the slobbered on bones back into the bucket. The drooped eye then fixes keenly on Bill as if he's the next course.

"Look, gents," Bill drags a wet-nap across his salty lips, "it's been swell. But either lay on the irons or take a walk. I'm eating."

Physical violence is a staple of Rauch and O'Reilly's

act. Real Old World artisans. So when O'Reilly fans out his overcoat like great batwings to shield his partner from prurient eyewitness accounts, Bill knows what's next. Rauch pulls Bill to his feet. His legs buckle like flaccid fire hoses. All his blood is tied up in the act of grinding the dead bird into pieces, the inward raspy teeth lining his stomach ripping into the chicken dinner like a thrashing shark. Every once in a while, a tooth breaks off, passes through Bill's colon and shows itself as a small triangle of serrated white poking through the skin of a turd. If Bill had had the foresight to collect the teeth lodged in his crap, by now he'd have a pretty nice shark's tooth necklace. Swell gift for a gal, once he'd bleached away the shit stink.

Rauch cocks an arm bigger than Bill's useless legs put together. From the angle of the pending blow, Bill's stomach is the target.

"I wouldn't do that if I were you," Bill warns, but the bruiser buries a fist right into where Bill lives, smashing into his world like a meteor striking the earth as choruses of angels croon a catchy jingle from his childhood, a ditty written to convince impressionable youth that starch and sugar equal love and understanding. Bite down on the spongy yellow cake and feel the creamy filling squirt into your mouth in an explosion of sexual innuendo and the hammering shame of unfulfilled expectations, that the moment you stop craving snack cakes is the moment life will tear you to pieces.

"I told you not to do that," Bill says with unconcealed satisfaction when he realizes his *other* mouth, the fast track to the colon, has externalized and taken hold of the flatfoot's arm. Bill sucks in his stomach, and razor sharp teeth scissor off Rauch's hand. The flatfoot wails louder than a siren as blood geysers from the jagged stump. His partner ditches the batwing routine and opens fire on Bill, who flexes his abdominal cavity and spits the severed limb in O'Reilly's face. Bullets spray haphazardly from the muzzle and tear through a Catholic youth group out on safari in the urban jungle. The saddest part of the whole affair isn't that Bill has burned another bridge or the loss of human life. Those things are inevitable. Nothing saddens Bill more than realizing the long the arm of the law isn't as long as it used to be.

3.
Rat Kingdom

Neon headaches, blurred faces and mile-high steel monoliths streak by in a panorama of discordant voices fighting for traction against the grinding wails of street hustlers and peepshow barkers steering traffic toward rigged games and salacious delights. Feet, don't fail me now! Trite even when applicable. Once Bill clears the final signs of bustling nightlife, he cuts between boarded up houses condemned to a date with the wrecking ball, and runs straight into a pack of goo heads at the end of their life cycle. Goo oozing from their pores lends the skin the glistening texture of tar reflecting the afternoon sun. Mossy teeth grind on silent tongues, the mindless automated jaw work of cows chewing cud, an echo of life before they crossed over. Not even a seasoned McRe can withstand the toxic effects of skin-to-skin contact with a goo head in such an advanced state of decay. This is not the end Bill had in mind. He imagined his big sendoff coming on the heels of a two-week binge. Wrappers and Styrofoam clamshells piled to the ceiling, every inch of his being caked in sallow grease solidified at room temperature. A motel turnkey shakes his head at the deplorable condition of the room. "Guess I'm gonna hafta clean up this mess," he says and commences stuffing garbage into dark plastic bags, starting with the bloated corpse at the center of the rubbish heap. After all, first things first...

A stray tabby yowling for a date distracts the goo heads long enough for Bill to slip the noose one more time. Close calls are getting to be a habit. But then so is everything.

The thirty block hike to Germantown is a study in the

shifting ugliness of urban environs, like walking up and down the verge of a salad bar in hell. Pavements gritty with salt. Wilted lawns. Continuous slabs of grainy gray meat paralleling the streets. We walk on spoiled food in cities constructed of prefabricated decay. An homage to the glaciers. Nature's eraser. Rubs away all traces of everything that came before. Someday even us.

The bakery windows are foggy, wet. The dogs of the manor must've been going at it. Not sex but siphoning each other's fat. Sex is a consequence of the need for sex. When you McRe, you need to McRe some more. Activities which interfere with the need to McRe are relegated then forgotten. Bill hammers on the locked door. An eternity passes before a listless figure emerges from the darkness to answer. "Damn, I just nodded off ten minutes ago." Pete yawns and scratches lazy circles on his belly, playing connect the dots with his siphon sores. The freshest of the bunch gapes at Bill like a bloody bat mouth. Somewhere, a cow is down a pint or two grazing in a field of other cows down a pint or two. Vampire bats leave their caves, blackening the skies. The sound of leather slapping leather blots out your every thought. Terrible to be out when that happens. Even more terrible if you're a cow. "C'min," Pete flaps his hand at Bill, "before we let all the flies out." Or let the bats in.

Bill scopes out the drifts of wrappers and greasy bags for Helga, Queen of the Desserts. "Where's your tastier half?"

"Out on business." Pete sniffs the air in hungry gulps. His nose has the fathomless dead reckoning of an experienced sailor navigating in a fogbank. The aroma of fried chicken sifts around Bill in undulating tendrils, strong as oily, cheap perfume to Pete's nostrils. "Lucky hotdog, you been restocking on the good stuff. Got a taste for the man of the house?"

Bill husks his coat at Pete like vulture wings fending off

the desert sun. "I'm dry. I had to hot-foot it out of the station empty handed. Bad scene involving the Man. Shakedown artists suddenly innarested in a follow-up on a random tip on that load I dropped off tonight."

"You lost me a mile back, Bill. What load?"

"Didn't Helga tell you I stopped by?"

"We ain't on speaking terms. Thinks I sucked a hit off of her without permission. How unspeakable does she think I am?"

"If she's a good judge of character, very." Bill sits on the floor before he passes out. His blood sugar falls with meteoric alacrity after physical exertion. Systemic metabolic upheaval has ravaged his body like the Mongols ravaged Europe, but with less panache and a heavier reliance on stealth. Bill inhales and exhales like a pearl diver before the plunge. "Point is," he says, short of breath, "the load bought the dairy, so the fuzz comes rolling in to finger me for tangential involvement in a fatal goo OD. I mean, what's the angle? Mine, theirs? *Ours*? Felt like they were pushed into connecting up dots that don't exist. Am I making any sense?"

With a dirty bare foot, Pete sweeps a clean spot on the floor and takes a seat, Indian-style. He's got a decade of youth on Bill, so he's still flexible in places Bill can scarcely move. "I sympathize with ya, one-hunnerd percent, but try to see it from the perspective of the law. Goo head population's been on the rise for a decade now. They gotta do something to address the problem. Who else are they gonna shake down 'n' harass? The mayor's fat-ass fifth wife or the governor's mistress? Eff no, they ain't going there. So that leaves grinding a boot heel on the necks of those denizens of society whose necks are slung lowest to the ground, the Bills and Petes of the world. Which is why we hafta stick together, amigo. Help yourself to a couple of wrappers. I'll take the air and see if I can dig up anything. Be willing to bet yours ain't an isolated incident." Pete springs to his feet, slides into open-toed shoes secreted away in the debris field. "Back in a jiffy. Whatever you do, don't leave. If the landlord catches this place empty for a second, the court will invalidate our sit-down strike. Goddamn laws make it tough on us all. Say, uh, I wasn't gonna say nothing, but you've got a little something on your shirt. Something *saucy*."

Pete ditches Bill at the bakery, a place he hates with a passion. The floors are the color and consistency of flour. The grainy feel of fine white powder crunches beneath your feet. No footing whatsoever. No air either. When the door shuts, it seals you in like a space capsule. And the rats…something has them up in arms and tails. The soft plaster walls bulge in spots where they wrestle each other for control of some valued commodity or hallowed space. Rats fight dirty. Teeth and claws, shivs and straight razors. Nothing is off limits in the rat kingdom. It is only a matter of generations before rats have the capacity to mix gunpowder. Then come the dynamite factories. Then A-bomb and H-bomb factories that crank out rat-sized bombs deadly enough to irradiate half the North American continent. A nervous UN security council extends the rats an invitation to negotiate peace accords and nonaggression pacts, a seat at the table of human progress. Big win for the rat kingdom. But during the meeting, a tac-team of UN exterminators barges into the room and wipes out the entire rat delegation. International incident unseen since a U.S. president vomited sashimi in the Japanese prime minister's lap. The secrets of advanced weaponry were the sole province of the exterminated delegation, so the rats regress to internecine feuds over scraps. Whatever. Just keep your paws off of Pete's wrapper stash and everything is five-by-five.

The rat wrestling halts suddenly. Bill's ears pop from

the change of pressure as the door opens. A surge of cold autumn wind blasts a hole through the paper dunes, kicking up a colorful storm that snaps and crackles like a thousand businessmen battling the morning newspaper. In waltzes Pete, and right on his heels come O'Reilly and Rauch. The door closes and forces air up the stale bakery chimney, stirring to life the sickly sugar residue of a million baked goods, chocolaty cookies and rich layered cakes heaped with frosting an inch thick, and doughnuts glazed and sprinkled, their guts bursting with jellies and creams. The stuff of florid dreams. But that was a thousand yesterdays ago. Today it's the stuff of dingy nightmares. Leftovers.

"How's the meat hook?" Bill asks with lackluster sincerity.

Rauch holds up the wad of bandages cocooning his right hand. So soft and delicate. Like mounds of shaved coconut and melted marshmallows. The coating for a Sno Ball. Bill's toothy stomach grinds at the toothsome thought of eating one. A Sno Ball that is. "Pulling a shiv on a cop." Rauch snarls like a rabid wolf. "That little stunt will net you a protracted date with a lifer, one queer for skinny boys. He'll give you something to do with that smart ass mouth."

"No weapon, no case, flatfoot. Unless you think I swallowed it or something. Or maybe I'm transforming into a monster. A regular beast of the night. Fangs, claws, hairy back. The works."

Pete gathers himself close to O'Reilly in furtive twitchy movements. Pete's been in the company of rats so long he's not only adopted their bad habit of eating each other but their body language, too. "See, what did I tell you? He's getting irrational. You better do something to straighten him out. I think my technique has lost its efficacy." A startled, jumpy shrug. "He's out of my league, okay. I'm bowing out of the case—at no expense to the uh department of course."

"You disappoint me, Mr. Winters." O'Reilly smiles at Pete, the grim smile of a wounded jackal. "And although the department appreciates comps, our policy on loose ends is shall we say inflexible?" There is a great and terrible pause before Pete gets a demonstration of the department's cauterization technique. Standard operating procedure to let the superfluous element comprehend his own superfluity, that he is expendable as a cockroach or a plastic trinket from a Midway arcade. Was there ever any doubt in Bill's mind that Pete worked for the Man? Yes and no. Bill's sixth sense for stool pigeons runs on a delay mechanism through which he can clearly see the ruse unfold in the precious moments *after* the stool pigeon's cover story collapses, which then signals the pre-temporal cortex of his brain to jump back in time and rewrite his memory of the episode as a foregone conclusion. Not a useful tool, but a tool Bill can nonetheless credit as one of his many valueless gifts. O'Reilly's expertise comes in handy, finally, when he snaps Pete's neck at the fifth vertebra. The light goes out of Pete's eyes like an empty oil lamp. His body falls into a mound of burger bags crisp with dried grease, some so brittle the impact blasts them to shards.

"Glad to see you made a clean break of it," Bill says, dropping a hint or putting in an order, however one wants to interpret a man's actions in the moments before his death. "I despise needless suffering. It's all so…needless."

"You ain't getting out of this that easy." With a pass of a silver wand, Rauch rockets Bill off his feet. That was the loving touch of a cattle prod Bill surmises from the buzzing in his ears and his teeth wriggling like worms on a July sidewalk. "You're coming with us." A second application sends Bill into a choking full-body spasm, the muscles contract so violently he loses control of his bodily functions.

"Asshole," O'Reilly yells at Rauch. "He shit himself.

Why do you always hafta overdo it with that thing?"

Rauch glares down at Bill writhing in the landscape of treasured garbage. There's murder in his eyes and a second element that strikes Bill as brotherly, biblical hatred, compassion with a little touch of envy. "I'm doing what's needed." Rauch recites a passage from a cop rulebook. Section this, paragraph that. Meaningless jargon seeped in doubletalk. But he's made his point. "Now shut up and get 'im in the car."

4.
Case for the Black Worm

At the station, a turnkey shoves Bill into a cell with a sink and toilet state of the art for 1920. "Clean yourself up, fuggin' animal." After rinsing his pants and underwear in the toilet, Bill watches the sun disappear behind the buildings as the bars draw mosaics of shadow on a cement floor gray as dead man's skin. It must be time for O'Reilly to call for him, which he does. "It's like two hearts beating as one," Bill tells the Irish flatfoot in a grating brogue. "All that's missing is a bouquet of flowers and a box of chocolates." Bill wishes.

O'Reilly hands Bill over to a lean, young functionary, hired muscle to take the load and liability off the department's back. "Put him in I–9," O'Reilly licks a dry split in his lower lip, "the Red Room."

The flatfoot wasn't kidding. I–9 looks like an abattoir bathed in cattle blood in the process of oxidizing. A lifeless, dead sort of red. A minute in there and Bill's eyes burn with hang-over intensity. He squirms in his red chair as if it's plugged into the main switch at the power company. An electric frenzy pulses through Bill. He can feel his skin peeling down to the bone, exposing the tendons and ligaments, like pink piano wires for the striking. He's keyed in all right. Dying one second at a time in the Kingdom of Red Death. Wasn't the last room in Poe's famous story painted a kind of dreamy, numb crimson as an ode to the plague sweeping the lands? Heavy-handed symbolism with Bill dying for a fix and all his straws confiscated by the Man. He could try putting the squeeze on an abscess. No good. Any pus mingles with the globules of adipose and the whole transaction's queered from the get-go. Cuts the effect in half, and a shot of the heavy yellow infected stuff cancels it all together. Total negation.

"Can a fella get a glass of water and some soda crackers?" he yells, but the chamber of horrors absorbs his request. The walls and ceiling must be lined with acoustic tiles to deaden sound. No better way to muffle his screams as the screws beat his kidneys with cakes of soap wrapped in pillow cases. He may piss blood for a year, but the reputation of the department shall remain squeaky clean.

Unrestrained by cuffs, Bill noses around the room to chase away the dark thoughts cluttering his head. Banal setup. Two straight-backed chairs. Rectangular table suitable for a flea market. A spot of lamplight cascading down from a ceiling fixture. Garbage can parked in the corner with its nose to the wall. Must've been a bad boy.

Garbage can?

Can he be *that* lucky?

Hugging the can to his chest, Bill rushes to the table and turns it upside down. What temptations have the chunky dumplings farting behind desks left for his pleasure? Cupcake wrapper? Doughnut box? A slice of uneaten coffee cake dropped on the floor? Must be something good. Police dumpsters have such choice pickings that since the McRe problem the coppers started incarcerating their garbage, too. Well, the *other* garbage.

Shit. Empty. Just his luck to drill a dry hole.

Bill puts the can back where he found it. As he turns it right-side up, he feels something inside shift. Something semi-solid. He sticks in his hand and glides a tempted finger along the bottom.

"Would you look at that?" Bill rubs a smear of black goo between rough scaly fingers. It's a mature patch. Gummy and noxious as asphalt. "You sure are a crazy sonofabitch to break your way *into* a police station."

"Taste me," the black goo suggests in a voice guttural and raspy as rocks grinding in a gizzard. "I know you've thought about it, wondered what all the hubbub is about. Go ahead and find out for yourself and *taste* me."

"Precocious little smudge, aren't you?" Bill stretches the small patch of goo like a lad stretching a piece of chewing gum from his mouth to the externalities of the world around him, testing the limits of its flexibility and tensile strength before letting it snap back into place. "Matriculated at the best schools probably, a product of social engineering, a carefully crafted upright member of society. Unreliable sources have spread vicious rumors that I used to be one of those. Not that I can remember. But if I close my eyes, I can feel a dull persistent ache in my bones. Residual pains from bearing the burdens of the world on my back. Bill is just a cover. They once called me Atlas, so I shrugged and the world fell away in the void. I had little choice, see. The terrific strain of it all, it tears you to pieces."

"Snap out of it, Bill. Don't let it get the best of you."

"Nothing gets the best of me." Bill wads the goo into a hard little marble and reunites it with the colony. "Only the worst."

"See it from my position, Bill." The goo's words bubble up at him like farts in a bathtub. "Taking the final step is paramount to cracking the case."

"Case," Bill's wonderment boils over, "what case?"

"The case, Bill. Have you forgotten again? You were employed by the department as a field agent. A provocateur. A spy."

"What about Pete and Helga?"

"Helga's just in it for the kicks. Pete's a run-of-the-mill CI. A paid rat whose usefulness had run its course. Rats have a limited lifespan. Some more limited than others."

25

"Understandable." Bill places the garbage can on the table so that the light beams down its mouth. An interrogation standard. But the goo colony reacts violently, begins to quake and shudder like a dog caught piddling on the rug. "Is the light too much for you to handle?"

"I'm fine, Bill. It's just my relatives prefer the darkness. Me, I can take or leave it. I'm flexible that way. Make some shade and I'll separate." Bill scoots the can until the colony is back in darkness, and a thin black worm detaches from the pack, inches out into the light and stretches its blank face upward, unafraid, regarding Bill with an undreaming emptiness, like a wad of formless clay begging an artist to grant it shape. "I know you like to see who you are addressing. Well, here I am, Bill. Address me."

"You gotta name?"

"No names, Bill. I don't want to queer the integrity of our relationship."

"Feels pretty queer as is."

"If you say so, Bill. I'm not here to take a contradictory position. I'm here to facilitate the final step of the investigation, to wit seeing that you sample the black goo. If you wish to conquer a thing, you must become it, Bill."

"Walk a mile in the other goo's shoes."

"Yes, Bill. If you wish to put it that way. This is your case after all. Total autonomy." The black worm arches its back then wavers to and fro like a charmed serpent. "I see greatness in you, Bill. The stuff of legends."

"Maybe. But being a legend means dying."

"A formality. You'll live forever in the annals of social progress, superseding the need for flesh. Besides, there's not much of you left to glorify. What are you up to? Five, six times a day?"

"Twice a day, tops."

"Another formality. You're all used up, Bill. Skin

and bones, and not much else. But there's a quick way to circumnavigate mortal limitations."

"How?"

"Eat me, Bill. Eat me and all will be revealed."

"But you're poison. I've seen what you do to people. They become mindless bags of shit."

"To the casual observer. But appearances can be deceiving. Take me for example. I'm a little splat of nothing. Yet the great Bill Vine, his lofty morals notwithstanding, commends himself to me as a friend. I have that effect on people, if they take the time to get to know me. Most would rather make a snap judgment based on pure externalities and superficialities, when all that counts is what's on the *inside*."

"You make a convincing argument." Bill sticks his hand in the can, making a perch of his index finger for the black worm to crawl on. "So you really think it's a good idea for me to eat you?"

"I wouldn't have it any other way. Think of it as communion, eating the body of Christ, as he *should have been* after worms tilled his flesh back into the black loam from which it came. Your salvation depends on it."

"Decadence has pushed me beyond the borders of salvation," Bill licks clean his finger, "but you knew that."

The black worm dissolves to a fiery patch of jellied gasoline dancing on the tip of his tongue. The red room fades to nerve-sparked messages scribed in dead languages undreamed of since the fall of the Sumerian Empire. Ancient symbols fall from the sky like cryptic snowflakes. Now is the winter of Bill's contentment. Solace in the belly of the beast. Nobody can reach him now or ever. He has passed through the veil of this reality and into a realm where God's arcane tricks don't apply. Bill hasn't cheated death. He has surpassed it. Rendered it an irrelevancy.

Long bony fingers make a play for Bill's flesh then

withdraw with sudden, overpowering revulsion. "What kind of game you playing here? This man ain't never had a pulse. I don't know what kind of two-bit outfit you're runnin' here, pal, but I don't deal in substandard materials."

Adios, pard'ner. You had your chance and blew it.

5.
Goo Head Blues

Bill passes through alleyways aglow with the soft lights of bed-sitters, insomniacs and entwined lovers. Cats hiss and rake their claws at him. Rats clatter over broken glass to avoid his lumbering footfalls. Mongrels bare yellowed broken fangs and trot off into the night. Gray and obedient, unbroken streamers of mist swirl around Bill's swollen ankles in gentle curls and eddies.

The change of seasons has cast a roasted, smoky veil over the city, a decaying succulence that draws him forward like Pan's pipes. Where is it coming from? he wonders with the dull agony of a dimwitted child. He's overcome by an unfathomable hunger. His stomach draws up violently into his body cavity. Ribs split the surface of the skin like shark fins slicing through open seas.

A young woman cuts the corner with her head down and bumps straight into Bill's pang-wracked body. Her fluorescent green eyes meet Bill's empty gaze, now fixed on her neck. Blood pumping through her arteries pulsates beneath the skin in small quickening bumps. She screams and retraces her steps. No loss. She's not what Bill's looking for. Bill's objective lives in Germantown. A voluptuous frau by the name of Helga, a woman known to cohabitate with rodents great and small. Bill's gray fingers fidget in his coat pocket, focused on a small barb of sharpened metal, metal with a bite to it. O'Reilly slipped it to him before releasing him on an unsuspecting public. Nonsense. The public suspects plenty. The public knows the score but chooses not to let that section of the newspaper sully their pretty minds.

A band of neighborhood delinquents pokes Bill with sharpened sticks, untwisted coat hangers, broken whiskey bottles. He lashes out with a surprisingly quick hand and catches one of the indistinguishable brats by his unshorn locks. His companions flee in haste. Bill's mind digests them as two dimensional objects, no more than cardboard cutouts caught in a gale and blown out of state, out of mind. What was he thinking just then? Unimportant. Bill has a new toy to paw and slobber on, something warm and *squirmy*. For a while anyway.

He arrives at the bakery. The door is locked. The significance of this passes through his mind like a hot wind through the ancient ruins of an undiscovered temple. Bite. Teeth. Metallic teeth. O'Reilly's key. Guided by patterns imbedded in the dexterous tissues of his hand, Bill inserts the key. The operation from hereon is as mystical to Bill as tribal rites of passage and the sacred rituals of a dead city trapped in liquid amber. The mutability of his thoughts concerns Bill. The endless permutations of possibilities are staggering yet also compacted, limited. A small orb that curves infinitely in on itself best describes the feeling. Inwardness falsified as outwardness. Slavery masquerading as self-control.

Bill finds the lady of the house both in *and* out. A long straw extends from her naked left hip to her slack, purple-blue lips. Helga's eyes are blank as boiled eggs, her body hard as a figurine carved from creamy white elephant tusk or a bone picked clean by scavengers. No matter. An atavistic hunger, ancient and aboriginal, boils in Bill's guts. Waist not, want not, Bill takes over where she left off, inserts the straw under his swollen tongue (not quite football sized, maybe a baseball; sports analogies are a sound medium to work in when dabbling in hyperbole) and starts the process of transference in wet, croaking glurps. Aztecs used to eat their enemies to gain their knowledge, believing spiritual energy to be some mutable commodity that one can ingest as easily as shit out. Savages didn't understand the human soul's imperviousness to stomach acid. It can only be softened and dissolved through a rigorous process known as living.

Helga tastes better than he remembered. A smoky finish with notes of Peanut Buster Parfait. What he can't finish he'll take with him. Do they make doggie bags as big as body bags? No. But Bill is no stranger to improvisation. Callous hands wring the uneaten portions forward like squeezing toothpaste to the end of the tube. The rest is the physics of applied pressure, Bill's dead weight versus the frailty of the exiting aperture. In one continuous wriggling spasm, a long albino worm streaked with red highlights slithers out of the pink hole and curls on the floor with the verve of a faceless jellied confection. Sweets from the sweet.

Bill returns to the alleyway where the amateur McRe crossed over. As restitution for depriving them of sustenance, he passes along a tip to a pack of vultures. Germantown. Bakery. Tasty snack. They thank Bill and wish him the best of luck with his new stigmatizing identity as a goo head. So what? Not as if his old identity carried any benefits of membership besides participating in the urban jungle's cycle of life. Vultures feed on McRes. McRes feed on themselves and each other. Goo heads feed on vultures, McRes and themselves. So many survival schemes absent any discernible scheme to survive.

A couple of thugs rubbernecking for fresh meat home in on Bill. His shambling locomotion simulates inebriation, a drunk asking to be rolled. More amateurs looking to punch out early. Must be something desperately wrong with this alleyway. It has a penchant for attracting losers. Bill reaches down into the dumpster and scoops up a thick wad of black goo pungent as Cleopatra's twat. The swelling and distension of his tongue presents a couple of hardships. Bill cannot wolf-whistle when a woman's skirt billows up to reveal her panties or the lack thereof. Nor can he consume black goo orally. That narrows his options to taking the low road, a nasty suppository approach, or the high road, shoving it up his nostrils to dissolve in the nasal cavities and drip down the back of his throat like viral congestion. Bill chooses the high road, as he lacks the requisite privacy to take a crack at the low road. The black goo drips down Bill's throat sweet as drawn butter. He snakes the white worm down to the inner sanctum of the dumpster, to the tarry bottom, so it can join and ferment with the extant goo colony. Cultivating new strains of goo is an art. But as all art is meaningless, Bill's reservations about making a monstrous ass of himself are negated.

The thugs get religion on the subject of Bill as a viable mark after witnessing what the average citizen calls a reprehensive act of self-annihilation. But what does the average citizen know about annihilation, self or otherwise? USA dropped two atomic bombs on defenseless Japanese civilians. One to stop a war. The other to see if the power of Christ had any pull in the Far East (Nagasaki Ground Zero was predominantly Japanese Christians). The annihilation of the Father, Son and Holy Spirit on a mass scale serves as exculpatory evidence presented to the court of public opinion, thus exonerating Bill's modest back alley self-annihilation operation. Bill should get a medal for limiting his low-altitude nuclear detonations to a targeted area not exceeding the size of the man named Bill.

A member of a neighborhood watch spots Bill and blares her police whistle. Goo head patrols, the stillborn brainchild of an anti-drug hysteric from a flyover state. Real Triple Crown asshole. Crucifix in one hand, Bible in the other, stars and stripes for a blindfold, he proclaimed the country's problems stem from a deficiency of moral fiber, as if the nation needs a bran muffin or a high colonic, which maybe it does, but if constipation were brains, that sparrow fart would be a Rhodes Scholar. Conservative closet cases of the world, heed these words: have your pipes thoroughly reamed and rodded before concocting social bromides in laboratories of hysterical fear.

Plumbers need to eat too.

An onslaught of wan outrage barrages him from both ends of the alley, lethargic insults and anemic gestures of protest. Population's heart isn't in it. Goo epidemic, scourge of the city perhaps. But fighting a scourge takes time away from couch vegetation in front of runway models pontificating on the state of affairs in thy neighbor's house, the howling dissonance of harlots, slapstick irrelevancies and spontaneous idiocies captured for posterity, to the chagrin of future scholars. Besides, there is no room for rebellion on a full stomach. Convenience stores are open 24/7 for the convenience of those *in charge*.

Bill slips through a group of gaunt bystanders he identifies as McRe gypsies, unaffiliated outsiders looking to lay down some roots. They give Bill the office, sly index finger slide along the side of a wide, hooked nose, as a signal that this is their territory now, and with Bill, Pete and Helga out of the picture, there's no one to challenge their claim. McRe power vacuums last about as long as ice cubes on hotplates. Bill does his morbid rendition of a smile and wishes them rots of ruck as he blends into the velvet folds of night in the City that Never Forgets or Forgives. Cold autumn winds shake scrawny trees into a knock-kneed skeletal frenzy, a cheap haunted house gimmick strictly from Squaresville, canned soulless ambiance underscoring how soulless an enterprise the world is. Bill plods through patches of damp curbside grass heavily mined with uncollected dog excrement. Nice touch, bonuses all around to negligent dog owners for making the city what it is today.

6.
Welcome to Negáshun

Hours of aimless plodding through acres of dried out dog links and shards of broken beer bottles and crushed water bottles, the landscape carpeted in rain-swollen cigarette butts and moldering litter left in the streets by average citizens, and Bill finds a goo head encampment at the edge of an industrial district. Real shithole. Amber fireballs belch out of listless smoke stacks. Unprocessed dust streaks the skies like an incurable gray sickness. No birds. No squirrels. No signs of life but for stunted trees and rows of electrified chain link fencing crowned in a menacing spiral of concertina razor wire.

A capitalist dream.

An attractive lady goo head clasps Bill's hand, and her palm vibrates in his like a telegraph stuttering out messages from afar, purely tactile communication, one mind plugged into another. In an act of spontaneous evolution, Bill's palm emits a continuous stream of words tickertape style, each character traveling along withered meridians once used to channel masturbation urges long since supplanted by unrelenting chemical longings. Good thing too. Lengthy explanations of ape DNA in the Vine family tree, to ease the social embarrassment of hairy palms, were really cramping Bill's style.

"So what's the attraction, dollface?" Bill asks and she points to a factory with windows blank and black as insect eyes, eyes that reflect the world's accumulated ugliness. Bill twigs the reason for the powwow immediately. The compelling odor of corruption encircles the factory like a halo hovering above the Purported Virgin (test results still pending; please check back in a couple of centuries). A stiff downwind breeze immerses Bill in a fleeting vision of a place where amber fingers of grain sigh and bristle at keen blue skies. White doves with eagle claws haul around sea turtles to drop on unsuspecting targets. White tigers shadow box polar bears in front of a packed house. Ringside seats worth ten large given away to shoeshine boys with pearly white teeth sharpened to points. The undercard ends when sandy beach towels soaked in high grade crude oil rain down and strike the canvas with a juicy splat. Referee calls it a draw. Shoeshine boys shriek in protest and demand a full refund. Tall men in yellow rain slickers produce awls, stab the boys in the left eye socket then eat the gouged out eye on a bed of contaminated Romaine lettuce. A mass coronation follows, proclaiming each boy the King of a Blind Kingdom. Short reigns all around. Every boy dies when a sea turtle dropped from on high caves in his skull. And the crowd goes wild. Paparazzi flashes blind the world for two thousand years. Management apologizes to the dead shoeshine boys then issues stale refund checks all around. IRS agents rush forward with sticky fingers to collect the checks as down payment on hefty bills for dying. "Nothing's free in this country, boys. Not even death."

"That was," Bill searches for the right word, finds the wrong one, "macabre."

"I've been expecting you, Bill."

"Oh? That's very innaresting. You're what I've been expecting, too. Long time since my last trip down the hole to wonderland. But please don't invite any rabbits to the expedition. I'd hate to accidentally kill one."

"Yes, that would be a hare-owing experience. I'm Poly. One L, as in many. The skulking shadow to my left is Henry K., abortionist. Holds the record for most unwanted babies scooped out in one day, fifteen hundred. Got called to the carpet by the Department of Ambivalence for flushing the aftermath down the toilet. Some of the aborted critters matured in the sewers and grew to enormous size. One swam up the pipes and sank its milk teeth in the governor of Kansas's prolapsed hemorrhoids. Now the ugly little shit bombs abortion clinics for K.A.D., Kill All Doctors, right-to-life radicals whose mission is to kill all doctors. Truth in advertising act's best work to date."

"Who are the others?"

"Extras in the drama of my life. I permit them to tag along, provided none of them step on my lines or chew the scenery."

"What's that make me? A guest star?"

"You always answer your own questions with questions? However can you stand being you?"

"Lots of practice." Bill takes a long sinister look at Henry K. He reminds Bill of the notorious south side jackroller Günter K. Deplorable enough stealing from drunks, Günter also cut off body parts as mementoes to impress ladies aroused by ghoulish acts. Worked about ninety-nine percent of the time. "I'd warrant the preservation of Günter's trophies was your doing." A furtive snatching glance at Bill tells him everything, and then some. Henry K.'s pupils run vertical as a snake's, a rare birth defect exclusive to the remote region of Switzerland where Günter was born. Proof that incestuous marriages and shallow gene pools are keenly honest. "Glad to know there's a croaker among us. Before long, all of us might need advice on preservation."

"I take it you're unaffiliated," Henry K. leans closer, exuding the sauerkraut passions of a criminally insane Nazi who dry clicks revolvers at babies, and sometimes the revolvers aren't so dry. "Strictly speaking, we never accept recruits, outsiders or tourists of any stripe. Natural born citizens only, which snuffs the need for passports, citizenship tests, swearing in ceremonies and immigration laws. All infiltrators are shot on sight. But I guess we can make an exception in your case. Doctored birth certificates are the norm for all citizens, so nobody will suspect that you're a *feelthy* infiltrator, although I will advise them to think otherwise. Welcome to Negáshun. Poly, be a doll and make him an appointment for a pasties fitting. Bill has the right body type for the queen of the Independence Day parade."

"No need, I brought my own."

"What we have here, Poly, is a true parrot, I mean patriot." Henry K. salutes Bill with an outstretched arm wreathed in an armband bearing the flag of Negáshun, a giant black minus sign inside a white circle on a red field. Any similarity to insignias associated with atrocities of the past is purely intentional, making the Negáshun banner a grand exception in the annals of human history.

National motto: Own Your Fuckups.

Capitol: Tetraminion. Population: unimportant (all meanings applicable).

The currency of Negáshun is the cipher, valued on par with the US dollar for reasons of complexity, inaccuracy and economic folly. USA borrows heavily from China. Negáshun borrowed idea of capricious monetary valuation from China. Ciphers look identical to US denominations but for hand-drawn minus signs under the noses of the luminaries portrayed. Negáshun's team of crackerjack pettifogs and ambulance chasers fainted at the thought of vandalized currency, but agreed the international fallout from suing a formative nation would outweigh the USA's need to exact petty revenge. For now.

7.
Open-Air Market

With Poly glommed onto him like a leech, who's to say if this is bad or good, Bill takes a riotous tour of Tetraminion's horrid open-air market, rated most unsanitary bazaar in the Western Hemisphere. Patrons are guaranteed to catch at least six incurable diseases per pound of goods purchased. Regulations, the scourge of commerce everywhere, have been outlawed. Restless spirits of tiny tykes suffocated to death in abandoned refrigerators give a rousing but muffled cheer from the Great Beyond. Vendors caught observing any sanitation or safety code, however innocent and reasonable, face summary execution by firing squad or three days in jail eating state-sanctioned offal.

Unregulated landfills skirting the market creep ever inward at the rate of ten feet per day. Residents at the fringes find themselves suddenly knee-deep in contaminated waste. Penalty for washing one's self is ten thousand ciphers or one month under house arrest inside house arrested by garbage. A glaring loophole permits the citizens to let a neighbor bathe them. Breathes new life into old maxim: you wash my back and I'll wash yours.

The largest section of the market is dominated by mendicants and sacred beggars supplicated on nail-encrusted soapboxes. The disembodied fluids of winnowed specters ooze down charming logos in pulsing streams as outlandish claims of snake oils endowed with magical powers saturate the air. Withered hands mock the motions of dehydrated birds pecking cracked earth for elusive traces of water. Broken beaks fall motionless. Dried out feathers crackle in the hot sun like crumbled cellophane wrappers. Iguanas dash out of holes in cruciform saguaro cactuses and strip the birds down to bare bones that spontaneously combust into pyres from which the birds emerge, renewed and whole. All that bottled potential for the price of one cipher. Will miracles never cease?

Bill exchanges a cipher borrowed from Poly for a bottle of snake oil. Until he can get a hold of a high quality laundry marker, he's stuck with worthless greenbacks. "What's in this stuff?"

"Black dreams," the one-armed peddler croaks in a dialect antiquated since one that afternoon. Granules of dirt speckle parched lips pulled taut over horrid yellow fangs. Real living fossil this one is. He reminds Bill of old-time rip-off artist Percy Doaks. Liked to run short cons on longshoremen. Queer up to a point. He wouldn't do the deed unless his potential partner could produce documents proclaiming their nether region had been AAA rated by S&P and Moody's. Big whoop. Rating agency whores would rate Babylonian whores AAA if the ancient gashes cough up the dough and promise not to cough up the account exec's private parts during culmination of the oral contract in the men's room at the Greyhound station. Brings new meaning to: "Ride the Big Grey Dog!"

Bill takes a hit of magic elixir and passes it to Poly, who drains the bottle in seconds. She buys three more bottles, drains two then gives the third to Bill. "Don't let me have any more or I'll lose my head and stir up a gangbang." Market square business grinds to a halt as Llumps, amorphous degenerates turned to mush from the excessive consumption of snake oil, ring Poly to audition for a role in her next intoxicated sexual explosion. Aided by three to six horrible wriggling pseudopods, Llumps ambulate by means of a sickening *schlup*. *Schlupping* has been known to induce revulsion and fear if seen in person, yet is considered uproarious if viewed on television or the silver screen. Before Llumps were permitted access to the hallowed halls of the entertainment industry (as laughing stocks in minor and often humiliating subordinate roles), actors performed in Llump-face, an elaborate costumed simulation now viewed as a racially insensitive abomination from unenlightened time. The late great leading man Thomas Blunder donned Llump-face for a tasteless roast that ended in fireballs of tragic death when one of the guests, a boozed-up old hag once thought to have been funny for about ten seconds in 1920, intentionally misconstrued the meaning of roast and set fire to the building to tell an awful joke over the smoldering corpses. "See, boys, now *that's* a roast."

8.

Gringe

A golf cart chauffeured by a Llump glides through the agitated crowd. Rampant whispers of rebellion are one way the citizenry ensures the government maintains its policy of perpetual apathy. Assassinations are also instructive but create the unnecessary expense of replacing one dead weight for more of the same.

"Finally, our ride is here." After they climb in, Poly slips one of the driver's idle pseudopod in the moist darkness between her legs, a classy way to tip while conveying directions silently along telepathic channels. Ripe smell of a transaction in progress motivates the flow of traffic to make a wide berth to avoid the risk of envelopment inside the ectoplasmic afterbirth of a spontaneously generated Llumpatto, the offspring of a lowborn male Llump and a normal, upstanding corn-fed female who needs to keep to her own kind and cease carnal exchanges with socially undesirable monsters.

Llumpattoes who pass as regular folks are often hired on the spot. Great jobs with full benefits, including gold key memberships to exclusive golf clubs whose front entrances are off limits to Llumps. "Back door only, Llumpy," the Llump doorman yells at the entourage of Llump cooks, waiters, bus boys, dishwashers and gigolos. All across Tetraminion, high-strung female executives swear on stacks of stolen Bibles that the sudden influx of Llumpatto brats bearing a family resemblance can be explained away by inexperienced Llump golf pros. "Every one of those *feelthy* cretins is plagued by the worst hook ever. Balls fly all over the place. So it's possible that one or more errant shots may have fallen down, ahem, the wrong hole."

In the wealthy sector of Tetraminion, green tentacles sprout from the ground, the tips anointed with rose blossoms speckled in pearly drops of black dew potent with the dark energy of an undreamed universe. The city looks different. Older. Eviler. Street lights run on the crushed, liquefied remains of trapped coal miners. Broken-hooved horses limp along cracked cobblestones soaked in bloody discharge. Long, cruel faces glare through unfocused windows. Pitiless men in tall black hats discuss setting the broken bones of poor children in splints hewn from the spiny limbs of Joshua trees. Scheming insects sing to victims of future criminal acts the nature of the crime un-culminated upon their person. Gray-skinned midwives drink deeply of red wine used to drown bastard sons and lodestone daughters. Llump lawn jockeys with the faces of wrongfully executed prisoners swing lanterns and chant ancient Babylonian curses to ward off creatures of unspeakable darkness. Three-legged dogs urinate on fences electrified to run up unspeakable electric bills. Blackened teaspoons clatter on silver tea services confiscated from Jewish families put to death for the prohibited act of shedding foreskins from trouser snakes, violation of Old Law dating back to the First Apple Orchard. Deplorable security. One sign written in disappearing sheep's blood warns poachers that, "Unlicensed pickers shall be prosecuted or persecuted, whichever comes most *naturally*."

The chauffeur decouples from Poly, thanks her for the swell tip and tells them there's no way he's stopping in this part of town. "Old money makes me ill," he says and shoves them out of the golf cart. The perfectly level pavement breaks their fall without a scratch. They hoof it to a nameless bohemian café overpopulated with out of work Llumps looking for a fast cipher. Grizzled men in dark rumpled suits run high stakes gambling operations out in the open. Pseudopod wrestling is the main attraction. Mangled screams rent the air as defeated Llumps bleed profusely from the ragged stumps of lost pseudopods, while the winners graft the spoils of victory onto their bloated bodies. Grand champions of pseudopod wrestling, those with fifty or more grafted limbs, retire to the lap of luxury washing dishes for the duration of lifelong contracts.

A hostess with beady eyes and clusters of hairy moles seats them at a corner table acrid with the stench of recent gunfire and sexual secretions. A Llump busboy *schlups* over to fill their teacups with premium snake oil. The rich scent of toil and death, blasphemy and idolatry trails up from the cups in restless, warlike curls. Poly drops in two saccharine tablets and mixes the concoction with a golden spoon. The tablets shatter, the spoon dissolves. Wails of disbelief rise from the café in tenebrous peals of woe. The patrons who witnessed the event are now cursed to wander forty years in the wilderness searching for a river to cross or a grave to crawl in. They draw holy signs in puddles of spilled ketchup and chant songs of the long journey ahead. "Tell me something fascinating about yourself, newbie. Lie if you have to. Any fool can tell the truth. But it takes a talented fool to tell a really entertaining lie."

"In the twilight of my youth I fell in with a professional panhandler named Rumford T. Mayfly, who kept a temperamental long-tailed macaque tethered to the world's most perverse organ grinder. It was a crude machine, shaped like a giant phallus. If he stopped stroking it for a second, the damn thing would go limp as a noodle, which drove the monkey into insane fits of rage. Seductive young ingénues affected by the pitiful sight of a monkey losing its mind would take turns straddling the grinder. Before Rumford knew it, he was knee deep in dollar bills, and the streets were suddenly flooded with homely businessmen making a homeward detour for lunch. Ten months later, the sidewalks were crammed with mothers wheeling around babies so ugly the macaque fled for fear of a class action claiming paternity."

"All very credible except the name of the panhandler. Whoever heard of a panhandler with a middle initial?"

A giant wad of Llumps locked in the frenzy of mortal combat tumbles out the door and rolls out into the street. By impure coincidence, a street cleaner decommissioned in the 1950s speeds by (its brushes swapped for rotating blades) and purees the Llumps into a toothsome paste called *gringe*. Big black tanker trucks roam the city on the lookout for meaty veins of unprocessed *gringe*. As if adhering to a schedule, such a black beast pulls parallel to the fresh *gringe* patch. Spotlights sweep the café in slow probing arcs as pinpoints of red laser light make all patrons honorary Hindu women. Fierce bulbous men in black hazmat suits exit the truck to hook up green rubber hoses rusty with blood from a thousand police interrogations. To cleanse the raw *gringe* of all *feelthy* adulterants, the hoses first spew essence of purity, a creamy white substance extracted from genetically superior races, then reverse polarity to suck up the processed *gringe*.

The spotlights go dark. The truck vanishes in a column of yellow sulfurous smoke that lingers for two and a half centuries.

Café business flourishes unaffected but for heinous accusations of rigged matches. The pit bosses compile the massive list of all complainants on Braille flash paper laced with cocaine and forward it to secretaries blinded for security purposes. A pass of hectic fingers and *whoosh*! every complaint is processed down to a fine white powder. Next day, the entire secretarial pool is dismissed for failing drug tests and a sudden spell of illiteracy arising from mysterious finger numbness.

On the heels of the *gringe* patrol, Henry K. storms into the café guarded by a heavily armed escort of Llumps drafted under Negáshun's mandatory military service act, which prohibits anyone taller than the tallest Llump from serving. All enlistees *must* have pseudopods, and homosexual tendencies are compulsory as per Don't Stop, Don't Stop, Please Don't Stop. Citizens of wealth and influence or their pampered offspring caught masquerading as Llumps (to subvert the enlistment requirement) suffer stiff penalties. Ninety days of conspicuous consumption at a luxurious spa living on nothing but vintage wine, crab cakes and beluga caviar spread on *gringe* crackers.

"Credible reports indicate this sector has been compromised by saboteurs determined to undermine truth, justice and the Negáshun way." Henry peers at them through tinted goggles, his hair swept back from his face in a grotesquely impossible comb under. "This is of course nothing new. But it does provide a wonderful excuse for dramatic and excessive displays of military might. Quick, get us to the Transport before all is lost!" The Llumps snap into action laying down suppressing fire, tossing grenades, kicking down doors, pistol whipping patrons and staff alike. The less opposition, the harder the Llumps fight. The café is leveled, smashed to bits, everyone inside processed down to hamburger. Black flags of caustic smoke jaunt skyward, knocking birds out of the air. Passionate cries of "hurrah for our side, hurrah for us!" are folded neatly into anthems and pledges fed into the sleepy minds of captive children.

9.
Ecunds

The firefight continues unabated to the boarding platform of the Transport, a monstrous black juggernaut some six stories high, a powerfully ugly, spiky contraption meant to induce fear and hopelessness not just in the enemy but in anyone connected to it in any way. "It's an experimental model designed to run exclusively on Llump power," Henry explains in low conspiratorial tones. "Rides choppier than a dinghy on stormy seas. However, it nullifies the possibility of running out of fuel in hostile territory. Tetraminion has *never* suffered a Llump shortage or a Llump embargo. More the pity, I suppose.

"This was originally a flying machine, but the damn Llumps couldn't flap the wings fast enough. So the project was repurposed for ground transportation. Notice the heavy chains. Not a safety regulation, as those are illegal in Negáshun. I suggested chaining the Llumps as an aesthetic improvement to spruce up the dreary atmosphere, and to elongate the lifespan of the crew. The hazards of freedom exact a hefty toll on the Llump constitution. It's a well-known fact Llumps in captivity live an average of twenty years longer than those in the wild. The most common cause of death among free-range Llumps is lynching. Although lynching Llumps is prohibited, it's nonetheless our number one national pastime. The Tetraminion Board of Llump Lynching financed the construction of a new Coliseum dedicated to the art of competitive Llump lynching. Big prizes awarded for originality, length of suffering, type and duration of choking burbles. That sort of thing."

The scenery passes by in weary stretches of yawning nothingness. Vistas of cracked, broken earth, dead forests and scorched underbrush unravel like crumbling scrolls locked in the desiccated darkness of pharaoh tombs. Drought, fires, erosion and war have devastated Tetraminion for so long nobody can recall with any clarity the prosperous times. Spotted hands webbed with soft blue veins sift through shoeboxes of yellowed photographs and pastel snapshots. Expectant mothers draped in gauzy veils of dust stare out dirty windows, awaiting delivery of telegrams from the future regretting to inform them of the loss of their son in the field of combat:

"Private So-and-So died valiantly. His sacrifice shall be remembered. You have our deepest condolences. This is just a form letter. We are not sincere."

Beribboned generals in camouflage tutus dance glorious jigs in front of Congressional committees convened to conclude nothing. None of the generals can recall anything of importance, not even the rationale for going to war. Blindfolded Representatives rush into the hearing to stamp APPROVED on unread bills written in the blood of children undreamed of. Congress unanimously funds the war effort for one more century. "But after that," declares the livid corpse of a Senator, his jagged crockery glistening with strips of flesh torn clean from the bones of widows, "we'll need to see definitive proof of progress; a couple of bodies to gnaw on should turn the trick."

The transport rumbles to a rollicking halt in front of Henry K.'s sprawling estate inside a gated community protected by Ecunds, a race of apish humanoids infamous for feigning public service in exchange for a glorified starter pistol and a shiny snip of tin shaped like a Star of David. Large brutish creatures with dark lifeless eyes recessed beneath primitive brows, Ecunds strike fear in the hearts of the citizens they are sworn to protect. The typical encounter with an Ecund ends in a tremendous bloodbath. Ten million acres of trees are consumed annually to process, file and disregard reports of bystanders maimed and killed during Ecund high-speed chases, random door-to-door sweeps and routine shakedowns. Night and day, the citizens live in mortal terror of falling victim to the Ecunds' propensity for violence. Answering the door is widely considered a profound act of bravery. The brainwashed, bullied citizens have signed petitions and sacred blood oaths demanding pay increases for the murderous Ecunds, less some unsanctioned element worse than the Ecunds fill the position for free. A mother of four (shot in the face for inadequate identification—stupid cow neglected to obtain two of the eighteen mandatory forms of ID) remarked to the *Tetraminion Times*, "If the Ecunds weren't on the job, I just wouldn't feel safe."

10.
Cabana Boys
& Monitor Lizards

"Nice little corner of the world," Bill muses over a glass of premium snake oil tinctured with lightning bolts drained from the testicles of storm giants. On every corner, street urchins fish for green pennies in nepotistic storm drains. Neighbors locked in fortified citadels sit in the numbing darkness taking turns inside iron maidens. "Please, let me feel something!" screams a frigid housewife. Emaciated alligators roam the concrete decks of marshy in-ground pools cared for by swarthy cabana boys in tight shorts. Stockbroker wives in loose fitting negligees tutor cabana boys on the correct use of skimming poles, both long and short varieties. Gentle hands glide down bulging shorts. Perfume of lust makes the boys faint and fall into the swampy water. Inspired alligators dive through scum to seize the boys by the legs. Great underwater struggles ensue. Hobbled boys emerge from the water holding alligator bags, shoes, belts and wallets. Sizzle of wet shorts flying through the air as the boys proclaim, "Today, I am a man!" The stockbroker wives wail cries of rape, and the Ecund infidelity task force storms the backyards. Slow motion shots of hot lead ripping through taut virgin flesh. Close-up on ragged exit wounds big as a beastly fist. Taking no chances, task force agents plant pistols with filed off registration numbers, pried from the cold, dead hands of lawful gun owners, in the cold, dead hands of ambitious cabana boys mowed down in passion's white heat. Dressed as a 1920s flapper in a smart sequined mini, the Ecund captain surveys the crime scenes in slinky wanton strides. "Pack these lads in ice before the flies curry the eyes. They are all mine, you seedy little pests." He lubricates a finger with a gob of spit and slides it deep inside the entry wounds, teasing each bloody aperture with a series of rapid then slow, seductive strokes. "Soon as one crime wave ends another one begins."

Henry K.'s silk lounging pajamas sizzle as he glides across the veranda to pour himself another glass of snake oil. "Poly promises to join us after she's paid off her sizable gambling losses accrued while playing license plate poker aboard the Transport. Llumps are terrible cheats. They superimpose, double-count, miscount and transpose characters, and have been known to use marked plates. There's an old saying in Tetraminion: never trust a Llump as far as you could stuff one down an incinerator. Which is not as far as you'd think."

"What kind of deviate entanglement is it now?" Bill asks with flagging curiosity.

"Poly's entertaining a 'night on the town,' a sexual odyssey inside a conglomeration of Llumps. The subject enters fully clothed and emerges naked. Llumps in coitus exude a digestive enzyme with a voracious appetite for polymers, cottons, wools, weaves and nylon. Harmless to flesh but wreaks havoc on a woman's misplaced self-esteem. Tremendous commercial potential. Dispersal of the enzyme into the ecosystem triggers a global-wide fashion meltdown. With no other options, fashion-conscious rubes drop billions on an experimental line of enzyme-proof clothing so impractical nobody can walk, recline, sit or stand without vicious cramping and general, persistent fatigue. Back, foot and mental problems arising from the unbearable apparel become so commonplace jet set divas devolve into gnomish hunchbacked monsters. The fashion industry disappears inside a year and is replaced with monitor lizard farms. Wonderful creatures. They get along smashingly with deformed freaks and can strut a catwalk with the best of them."

11.
Versing

Henry K. takes a seat on the crested rise of a red Turkish divan that once belonged to silent-movie star Clara Bow. "As a child, I adored her films. The flirtatious disaster written in those ferociously maudlin eyes said more in a glance than all the words in the dictionary." Warbles of nostalgic grief escape Henry like pent-up gas. "But when she opened her mouth, out bellowed the nasally guff of a Brooklyn bawd looking to stir up a gangbang. When there was no more golden silence for her to hide behind, the shadows of madness swallowed my sweet Bow. Those wonderful eyes sentenced to everlasting darkness behind the walls of a booby hatch. It's a grim ending for anyone, let alone a legend.

"It's a little known fact that she was a master of versing, also known as the art of thought absquatulation. Extremely popular among Amazon basin savages. Advanced practitioners can replace thoughts and realign subjective reality over unthinkable distances through telepathic networks piggybacked on the brainwaves of perceived inferiors. The Tetraminion military has been tinkering for decades with the most diabolical versing technique of them all, the linguistic swap.

"Imagine everyone in Russia wakes up tomorrow speaking Chinese and vice-versa. Nobody can read the signs or order off a menu. Tormented shouts of confusion echo up and down boulevards clogged with ten miles of traffic accidents. Nuclear mishaps take out major metropolitan areas. Paralyzing culture shock tinged with radiation sickness causes mass hysteria. Mental hospitals fill to the brim with self-diagnosed paranoid schizophrenics, almost all of them members of the mental health profession driven mad from ten-hour psychotherapy sessions in front of a mirror. Barricaded citizens sort out the confusion by convincing themselves they are double agents who've gotten so lost in their cover that reality has fractured. Solution: commit suicide, as prescribed in an incomprehensible spy handbook they cannot find. Leaders of both nations organize an emergency conference whereupon they agree the most judicious solution is for citizens of both nations to swap homelands. At the precise midpoint of the migration, versing agents exchange the swapped languages for an indecipherable Pig Latin dialect that incorporates twangs on a Jew's harp, interpretive dance and Semaphore. I know it sounds imminently impractical, immoral and abominable. But then that's what they said about concentration camps."

12.

Ectoplasmic Obscenities

Horrid screams of pain rise up from basement.

"Oh, not again." Henry snaps on a ratty pair of latex gloves contaminated with the gore of a thousand nullified mistakes. "It's nothing I can discuss openly, patient confidentiality and all, but that incredible slut Poly is knocked up with yet another batch of Llumpattoes. I've got," he consults a gutted wrist watch stopped at two minutes to midnight, "one minute to scoop out the little invading bastards before Poly has to stand in line at the Tetraminion Department of Misfortune and explain why she doesn't qualify for forced sterilization. Not yet in any case."

The *feelthy* abortionist takes the shortest route to his immoral rendezvous by throwing himself down a defunct dumbwaiter shaft that empties into a loathsome, unsanitary, unsanctioned operating theater. Damp, quivering colonies of exotic molds stage epic battles for limited resources. Vaudeville trained Llumps in nurse uniforms whip sensitive instruments and rusty scalpels at each other to test the unlicensed doctor's tolerance for horseplay. Some of them toy with Henry's new reverse autoclave, a machine designed to culture stronger and deadlier strains of bacteria to serve as a disproving ground for adulterated subspecies of penicillin intended to cure nothing but chronic cases of anemia unique to a physician's bank account.

The bogus nurses cease their dangerous hijinks to restrain Poly on a bloodstained butcher block crawling with buzzing black flies. Groping pseudopods spread her legs in a violent scissor. Henry anoints in his hands in a baptismal font used

53

to breed mosquito larvae, then shoves a fist deep inside Poly and begins to pump in and out like a tandem of lumberjacks overjoyed to destroy habitats sanctified by environmentalists more so than owls. "The objective of a prenatal beating is to traumatize and shame the ectoplasmic obscenities into self-aborting. If the detestable things stay the course and opt out of the comforts of oblivion, they shall have to endure the stigma of dark circles around both eyes for all their goddamn impotent lives. Nurse! Where're my golf clubs? There are eighteen other holes I'd rather be puttering around in than this one!"

A tidal wave of *feelthy* ectoplasm volcanoes out of Poly's cunny and catapults Henry grudgingly into the Modern Age. The millions of disadvantaged blobs swimming in the ectoplasmic stew make a mad *schlup* for the stairs. Dim chants of "free at last!" drift through the operating theater and down through the ages to mingle in the unconscionable rot of misappropriated Amendments.

"We've got runners!" Henry K. sounds the alarm. Deafening claxons soar above the fleeing blobs like birds of prey. "Get the bombers in the air, stat! Lazy Llump dogs aren't worth the cost of a bag of Llump chow!"

A squadron of model B-17s carpet-bombs the operating theater to a blackened lunar wasteland. Dresden's finest moment reenacted to HO scale perfection. The Llump nurses scoop the scattered, fragmented, nameless hunks of charred ectoplasm into pipsqueak coal bins. "Have those boys shipped to Newcastle at once. Can't have the next batch of recruits knowing what transpires in the field. The truth puts a damper on business."

Always the showman, for the finale Henry thrusts a lurid pink cutlass deep inside the catacombs of Poly's traumatized twat, rotates the deadly weapon in absentminded swizzle-stick swirls, and withdraws it with the flourish of a magician pulling a habit out of a rat (clever rodent liberated it from the Mother Inferior and stashed it up his ass). "Just as I thought," ghostly fingers shake the sword like a thermometer. "Down a quart. I recommend an immediate transfusion. Use only top of the line snake oil or your chasse will rust. So which route shall we endeavor? Rectal, anal or up the ole corn chute? Nurse! Show Mr. Vine to the lavatory, er, pardon my stutter. I meant laboratory. He'll have to administer the transfusion. I've got pressing business across town. Dame Margaret Havasham's cancer benefit is tonight. It's the newest thing in sickness aversion therapy. Cancer patients with lapsed medical insurance prepare a lavish gourmet banquet for the benefit of the *haut monde*. No more free rides for the metastasized masses. Poor doomed bastards wait tables, provide all the entertainment, and cleanup afterward. The treatment hinges on the cancer cells, a bunch of lazy fornicators, turning on each other rather than suffer the indignities of a little unavoidable exploitation." Henry bows at the waist, throws a kiss to a mural depicting Pat Nixon's passive acceptance of Vietnam War atrocities, and exits the operating theater on the world-weary shoulders of Llump bearers.

13.
Limo Ride

After an extensive snake oil transfusion, ten bottles of the good stuff, Poly is restored to her former glory as the Queen of Twilight's Last Gloaming. A retinue of Llump handmaidens and ladies-in-waiting confer the ornaments of her office: a crown of burlap woven from condemned surplus, an iron pyrite scepter encrusted in cubic zirconias and a pair of corrugated cardboard slippers stiff as Caesar's mummified pecker. "Welcome home, your majesty," Bill genuflects until his nose is submerged in the simmering, congealed swamp of decaying bodily fluids—vomit, blood, ejaculate, tears, pus, spinal leakage and brainpan seepage—a lifetime's worth of butchery and lust soaked into the pores of the basement slab, now soaked into Bill's enlarged, receptive pores, a new element for him to absorb and integrate into his being. "I think we should crash that shindig Henry ditched us for. Teach the tired old bore a lesson he'll never forget but never remember."

In a moment of inspiration, the most dangerous of moments historically, Bill and Poly pawn Henry's finest treasures—totem poles carved by tribes redacted from the pages of history; a bust of Pallas smeared in the droppings of plutonian visitations; the bones of dead kings plucked from the sharp beaks of noble profiteers; giant monochrome canvasses empty of meaning but full of opinions; mangled calamities of ego-infected metal—in exchange for the cost of chartering downscale transportation for an upscale event, a stretch limo operated by a disreputable Llump livery service. The passenger compartment stinks of regurgitated vodka and infected sores. The floorboard littered with used hypodermics and empty goo ampules. Sharing the ride with them is a bloodless creature of the road, an Old World junkie sporting the narcotic, disembodied grin of a sainted huckster, the type capable of selling water to a drowning man. Not the kind of person even a goo head wants to rub elbows with. Real slippery cretin out on a toot, thinks he can impress other addicts with extreme acts of exotic drug abuse. Today's road-show features the revolting habit of sucking orange peels dipped in Sterno. Ancient gimmick strictly from cough syrup.

"Try some," he insists and opens a mayonnaise jar brimming with gelatinous blue gunk. "You hafta supply your own fruit. I sold the last of my roadside citrus to a lean exec in tailored threads. He flashed me a piece of wrist hardware that cost more than the gross product of Tetraminion then slipped me a twenty for six bits worth of citrus, so I asked, 'What's the catch?' and he said, 'Jack 'it off.' I told him sure thing and whipped out my meat for a thorough thrashing. I may be old but I can get it up in a Negáshun second. Furious wrist action and lots of spittle helped me spurt in about fifty seconds. When I finished, I looked at him for approval, and he's paler than a bleached albino. 'Not good enough?' I asked and he mumbled something about getting away and carjacking, so I bashed him over the head and stole his car, too. Strange cat, I thought, until I remember I was wearing a nametag that said Jack.

"Name's Gilgamesh. My friends call me Mesh. You can call me Ga, like an infant's coo. Hard to believe I used to be one of those. Does that make me a cynic? I guess so. The world needs those as much as it needs dry cleaners, prostitutes and gumball machines." Ga sucks maverick splotches of Sterno from his horrid blue fangs. "I personally detest Llumps. My daddy was a Llump humper. Broke mama's heart. I'm probably half-brother to sixty percent of the Llumps in town. That's why the Llump driving this wreck picked me up on the side of the road in exchange for nothin'. We're family, and family sticks together. Last night, there was a shooting in Llump Town. No prints on the gun. Just traces of Llump DNA. So the Llump DA has Judge 'Hang 'Em High' Harrison, a big-time *gringe* eater, issue a bench warrant for the arrest of any Llump unlucky enough to be in the vicinity of the cop holding the warrant. Far as medical science (as refracted through the System) is concerned, all Llump DNA is identical. Subtle differences between genetic markers, blood types and alkaloid levels in pseudopod slime are an inconvenience to the courts, who don't feel it's their responsibility to sort out lowlifes biologically indistinguishable from one another. So the bailiff slaps the cuffs on the Llump DA, who pleads *nolo contendere* and begs the court to send the *feelthy* murderous scumbag, that being himself, up the river for life."

The limo plows through a procession of blind nuns and crippled Llump children on their way to midnight mass. Beggars scramble into the streets to pick the pockets clean, taking everything, crosses and undergarments, sanitary and soiled. Vultures descend from the blackened sky to pick the bones clean, taking everything, meat and guts, untainted and diseased. The authorities arrive to collect the stripped, anon remains of the John and Jane Doe's. The case closes of its own volition. The paperwork disappears in a puff of acquiescent smoke.

"Sometimes prayers *are* answered," Ga whispers in Poly's pearled ear, as he rubs Sterno on the insides of her thighs crawling with dark branches of varicosed veins dried to the consistency of diamonds. A surge of latent ectoplasm jets out of Poly's snatch and dissolves the tired old junkie's hand to a puddle of nacreous slime. "Fuggin' Llumpwhore!" Ga yells, cradling the negative space of his un-hand. The Llump limo driver slithers an unoccupied pseudopod through the partition and absorbs the pink slime into his pigmentation, gaining instant acceptance in social circles that once considered him less than dung. His ancestral credit ratings soar. Posh estates, stocks and bonds fall into his lap. He attends a polo match to exchange tales of downsizing and insider trading, and to discuss the decorative virtues of gold-plated garbage cans and elephant leg umbrella stands.

Ecund cruisers flank the limo to escort him and his honored guests to the party. Pneumatic bimbos in French designer dresses hook arms and pseudopods with the driver as he *schlups* down the red carpet. Bathed in the flashbulb adoration of a million vicarious yearnings, he approaches the entrance just as the pigmentation shift wears off. The bimbos scream and throw themselves in front of moving subway trains. The event promoters all take jobs as cum scrapers in Argentinean bordellos. The Ecunds beat the driver into a sticky blob of *gringe* then charge him with impersonating a person of distinction. The Ecund commissioner flies to the scene of the crime in a single engine aircraft commandeered from a South America dictator, an experimental model that runs on ground-up coca leaves and the tears of homeless orphans. He scrapes the *gringe* blob into a vial and plugs it up with a champagne cork popped New Year's Eve 1963, the moment we entered the deepest and darkest chapter of so-called human *pro*gress, that first fatal plunge into the year it was decided civil rights should be conferred without exception upon the masses, as if the masses have the slightest inkling what civility is.

14.
The System

The commissioner slides the vial between anonymous folds of flesh, to keep it warm and safe and away from the prying eyes of wooly-headed liberators. Stately hammers fall on disks of exotic hardwood without making a sound as judges gag everyone in the peanut gallery, the audience currently blindfolded and shackled to dust-choked libraries of precedent and decorum dedicated to the preservation of unwritten sacred traditions. Case closed ("As if it was ever really open," the bailiff chortles to the stenographer), the vial is stashed behind lock and key to languish in the company of a million identical vessels of ill-repute, each enumerated and cataloged and sorted for processing within the System, which is an end unto itself, and a dead one at that.

The System has no revolving door policies. Once you are in the System, you are in it forever. The System never forgives, forgets or exonerates, for no such function has been built into the System.

The System is a reflection of those who built it. Impassive, gray men in deteriorated black robes ripe with the stench of death. They have the uncanny ability to stare for hours at a piece of dangling string and then, without hesitation or reflection, jump to their feet and tie it around the neck of a stranger whose history is to them of no importance. "The holes in the earth must be filled with *something*!" they declare. That holes in the earth, in the moment of creation, are empty is an unconscionable disgrace to the System.

Structures within the System must have purpose and that purpose, once invented, must be fulfilled to the utmost, lest the System stop making things bereft of purpose. The purpose of the System is to promote the purpose of those things the System has blessed with purpose. To condemn the System for an act of purposelessness is to condemn the System itself, so the System shall always find a purpose for all things within its sphere of influence and those things which *appear* to be within its sphere of influence. Appearance supersedes factual relationships to the extent that pursuing such appearance benefits the System. Any appearance deemed harmful to the System is automatically attributed to provocative elements out to demean and disparage the good name of the System.

Never in its history has the System admitted any wrongdoing, nor is any agent of the System empowered to admit wrongdoing by action or forbearance of action. Any agent of the System caught directly or indirectly implicating the System via action or inaction, or thought or forbearance of thought shall be brought before the System for immediate absorption, assuming any portion of the agent remains unassimilated from said prior engagement as an agent of the System.

Total assimilation into the System does not guarantee immunity from the System. The System reserves the right to re-assimilate the assimilated when and if the System deems such re-assimilation is warranted or, in certain cases, when it is unwarranted. The System cannot be held responsible for the actions or inactions of the System. That the System acts at all or chooses not to act is at the discretion of the System.

The autonomy of others is a constant threat to the System. It is the System's position that all autonomous actions should be first approved by the System, for if any autonomous action should result in an outcome unfavorable to the System, the System will seek to rectify said outcome to one that favors the System, even if such rectification results in disproportionate hardships inflicted on the autonomous actor.

The System is not predicated on fairness or proportionate justice. The System metes out what it metes out in whatever portions, allocations and distributions it sees fit to apportion. That some should suffer more than others is by design. The System's first imperative is to ensure the structural integrity of the System. If the System were geared to evenly spread suffering, the System would collapse inasmuch that the System, as it exists today, would cease to be. As the System has never been recalibrated to allot suffering in an even fashion, it is unknown what ill-effects and contraindications would threaten the viability of the System. But suffice it to say that if such an experiment were undertaken, the System would change, and by virtue of such changes would no longer be the System, and if the System no longer recognizes itself, the System is hereby empowered, in name of preserving the System, to destroy those who changed the System. So saith the System. Amen.

15.
Vargas Bulba

Ga runs screaming from the limo, crying after his liquefied flesh, begging it to return and reconstitute with its master, as if his maverick molecules were a lost pet. "Adios, pard," Bill says with a pained Jericho smile as he and Poly slip unnoticed through holes in the Ecund dragnet and crash Henry's party as planned.

The Llump doorman stops Bill in the foyer. "Proper attire only," he admonishes then holds out a gold jacket adorned with a coat of arms, a bull elk impaling an African boy in a loincloth, the star-spangled midnight of the boy's face frozen in a priceless look of surprise as the elk stabs him in the groin, the many points of the antlers tearing open his abdomen and spilling his guts so they drape comically over the elk's muzzle like ten pounds of link sausage. "It commemorates the Golden Age of *gringe* consumption," the Llump explains, and after a mild protest, Bill takes the jacket, turns it inside-out and tosses it over a shoulder like a prep school lad hurrying home after a long day of exceptional education paid for by wealth dating back to the Middle Ages. Diamond tiaras and emerald tie clasps turn to face Bill and raise their glasses in toast.

"You're a smash hit." Poly adjusts her poison ivy boa so the shiny leaves capture the icy drip of chandeliers melting in the suffocating blast-heat of pointlessly diabolical banter concerning vivid mass genocide schemes and eugenics programs, consortiums on bypassing the ethical muck-and-mire of performing medical experiments on underprivileged children, convoluted speculations as to the most effective way to flood mass transit systems with sarin gas, the social benefits of dosing soldiers with venereal diseases, and bombastic recitations of barbaric doctorial theses postulating the rapidity of goiter development among the lower classes if deprived of iodine.

"Without pure research, *pro*gress would grind to a halt," boasts Tetraminion's Surgeon General, Vargas Bulba. His soft, vulgar lips are always stained ghoulish copper green, the result of siphoning the bank accounts of unwary patients. With surgical precision, his well-scrubbed pink fingers pluck an olive from the bottom of a test tube sponged from a promising cancer-drug trial, two years of crucial data spoiled for a cheap demonstration of manual dexterity. "Not that we plan on ever curing anything. But it does give the chronically ill a false sense of hope. I mean, do the cancerous rubes expect the medical profession to forgo monumental profits in the name of saving a few measly lives?

"Speaking of which, did you get a load of Lady Carrington's post-suggestion outbreak? I traced her case back to the Great Nypho, Negáshun's most notorious hypnotherapist. Unethical cretin placed a posthypnotic suggestion commanding the old split to come down with a serious case of shingles every time she called for the servants. I warned her to dismiss the staff for a few days until the hypnotic hold weakened. Predictably, the fading gash rebelled, and for a week straight she ran the help ragged doing everything for her, right down to wiping her unmentionable parts, which are even more unmentionable than last year. Now the old bat's sagging carcass is covered in welts the size of cherries. And if you must ask, and I know you must, yes, it was I who put the Great Nypho up to curing Lady Carrington of her hypochondria, for there is no more efficacious cure for hypochondria than a profanely bad illness."

Cancer victims in starched white suits tow leaden IV stands as they troll the crowd ladling sumptuous treats from great buckets like chummers baiting sharks. In a violent frenzy, respected figures in places of high authority thrash around the dance floor and snap at anything that moves or doesn't, insatiable animal hunger dominating all rational thought. Straight razors drawn from concealment flash through the air like sailfish leaping through foam-topped waves. Arterial sprays fine as atomized perfume-mist paint pink haloes on gilt walls. Select pockets of the melee break off into impromptu orgies planned months in advance. Pig-piles of writhing bodies exude moans that fall just shy of ecstasy. "This is fun!" yelps a woman who hasn't felt a tingle of joy below the waist since 1969. Her husband nods at her in lazy confirmation, then detaches his withered pecker, places it severed-end down in a glass of a fifty-year-old Scotch and watches with baleful, glassy eyes as brown liquid wicks up the jerked shaft and revivifies his member. He reattaches the whiskey-engorged dingus and shoves it deep inside his numb wife's lower catacombs, voted the most hopelessly sad spelunking site on Mother Earth. "This is fun!" she reiterates to rebuff her husband's pie charts and Venn diagrams illustrating that she's a hopeless liar. She plans to live the high life, whether or not her familiarity with the living can be verified.

For a cheap laugh, Vargas Bulba prescribed the cancerous servants a Ringer's lactate drip laced with his own special foul concoction: bilge water drained from ballast tanks of decommissioned aircraft carriers, syrup of ipecac, emetic powders and Tabasco sauce. The wait-staff collapses to the ground in convulsions. Respected physicians buy lottery tickets speculating which words the dying will scream during the epileptic fits. Most of the bets are on "help me." Opportunistic infections flee the dying for the Postoperative

Promised Land. Cold stillness settles down into the bones of the room, a feeling of contraction, as if the boundaries of the world were redrawn to reflect the fears of claustrophobics.

Up in the wastelands of the balconies, eradiated denizens crawl out from under dusty seats to survey the carnage from the safety of staggering unimportance. The scythelike wings of airborne scavengers slice through the stale, re-circulated air in morose husks. There is little to feed on that has not already been picked clean by larger, more powerful predators, not enough to fill an urn, let alone an oblong box. A lone figure stirs among the prostrate bodies. A waiter whose cancer has gone into full remission as the result of Vargas Bulba's "fully sanctioned and exceptionally ethical treatment," as per the legal deposition entered into the diseased organ of record by a baboon notary public with a "soft spot" (nickname for the baboon's Swiss bank account) for the medical profession.

In the coming months, the lone survivor forms the Church of Shit Happens, a revivalist movement that worships inexplicable survival tales as profound proof that God loves us the same way dogs love fire hydrants. The Church stages weekly contests challenging the devout to squeeze blood out of a turnip. "I have faith that one day," the preacher's voice blasts out across the congregation in humid waves of unrelenting skepticism, "we will discover a tuber capable of donating to the Red Cross! And if you'll believe that, here's a flavorless cracker that turns into human flesh once consumed!"

16.
The Complex

Unauthorized tour guides line the halls of the swanky ballroom, all of them brazen, unabashed panhandlers. The most forward of the lot, a Llump in a florescent-pink tuxedo, gloms its pseudopods onto Bill and drags him away from Poly. "This building has great architectural significance," he says with the condescending lilt of a museum docent who has eaten nothing but mummy guts and Sanskrit for a thousand years. "The foundation was constructed in the tradition of the pyramids. Each block of stone cut from the living rock and dragged along craggy terrain by disposable slaves. The losses were exceptional. The builder and its financier went belly up but were bailed out by government interventionalists with a soft spot for merciless venture capitalism. That'll be ten ciphers, please."

"Thanks," Bill stuffs a twenty in the Llump's breast pocket, "thanks for everything," and plunges down an interconnected sprawl of unmarked chambers, antechambers, niches, alcoves and nooks. It seems to go on for miles but occupies no more than half a city block. Families dangle over each other, suspended in hammocks hung inside recesses no wider than an innuendo. The clash of cooking odors overwhelms the senses. Outmoded artisans in tattered coats stand in doorways smoking pipes carved out of callow dreams. Children play doctor in the dark silence of unlit utility closets full of unlabeled caustic chemicals. Pregnant girls with steel hooks for hands prod the unborn to stop kicking. Asthmatics wheeze through dented harmonicas in tinny, strangulated woofs. Copulating robots clank in underground tunnels as malfunctioning radiators ejaculate scalding steam in the faces of untrained technicians. The enfeebled stares of veterans shine through cracks in crumbling walls compromised by carpet bombing during a Great War (which Great War is debatable). Dead pets rot at the bottoms of neglected cages lined with unread newspapers. To ward off bad spirits, the tenants nail up old gym socks stuffed with burnt coffee grounds, rotten eggs and an unaddressed jury duty summons applicable to anyone who touches it.

The complex contains seventy-eight liquor stores, fifty-six pawnshops, sixteen chop shops and one DMV whose waiting line stretches from 1956 to the End Times. Tetraminion's voter fraud law, passed in secret under cloak of night, requires certain registered voters in certain districts (although to whom the law applies has been left unspecified, everybody knows who they mean) to register at the DMV for the opportunity to obtain an appointment to obtain a Continuously Updated Picture ID (CUPID, but without the love-bug arrows) powered by the newest in Cortex Invasion Streaming Technology (CIST, but without the hope of remission), which pinpoints the whereabouts of certain voters to ascertain whether or not certain voters, based on their habits (what kind of lowlifes they associate with, what shops that cater to the lowborn they frequent), should, under any circumstances, be permitted to vote on Election Day, which, according to the law, can crop up at any time, day or night, without warning.

A palsied geriatric shuffles down the hallway alerting everyone that the Negáshun House of Patricians has called a no-confidence vote. A hand coated in a membrane of brown spots clutches Bill's arm and pulls him closer like a dying man eager to croak his final words to a witness. "Th-the H-House has l-lost all c-c-confidence in the n-n-nation's ability to p-p-practice democracy, and in-in-in itself," the old-timer tries to explain, but he's so hampered by stuttering pauses the meaning of his message crumbles to gibberish. Someone slips a cloth sack over the old timer's bobbling head, quieting him, as a drop cloth over a cage would shut up a yammering parrot. The responsible party is a second old timer, a less worn-out model with soft, runny eyes and buttery hands, the hands of a man who has never endured a day of thankless, back-breaking toil for a paycheck so minute, a microscope balks at its existence; a man who has never been basted in his own stink and the stink of others for twelve hours straight, never had to labor in breathless, confining darkness, never heard the devil whistle in his ears a thousand feet up on the edge of naked steel or watched decades of repetitive, robotic motions swell his knuckles to the size of golf balls. He has been sanitized for his own protection, but not ours.

"It's been a long night. A few soda crackers and a peck of water should straighten out Franz." After listening to the old, stammering parrot, the soft, runny old timer's soothing voice goes down smooth as honey. Bill hopes there aren't any ants around to spoil the picnic.

"What's your name?" Bill asks, and the old timer pauses down into the question as if he's not stumped but at a loss for a rational answer.

"Today, I'm Polaris. Tomorrow, who knows what I will respond to. Nerve damage suffered as a child at the hands of a *gringe* addicted father. There is no cure for my condition. Every day of my life, I am cursed to reinvent myself. If we meet tomorrow, I will have no recollection of this meeting, except if subpoenaed by a congressional committee. Funny how it works the other way around for everyone else. I hope the election turnout is sufficiently low. A high turnout, say ten to twelve percent, will force the House to declare the election rigged and ask for another vote. But a low turnout compels them to accept the genuineness of the vote, provided each and every incumbent, with or without a pulse, gets reelected."

The entire complex rises as one, busts through doorways cloaked in faded tapestries and tries in vain to chase down the dwindling outline of a speeding semi-tractor trailer, their designated polling place which never stops or breaks for anything or anyone and has been responsible for an untold number of vehicular homicides. The *Tetraminion Times* tried to publish photographs of the mangled dead, but Negáshun's President, a dented muffler wrapped in a swatch of purple velvet, declared the dissemination of such trashy pictures a violation of the deceased's constitutional right to anonymity, save formal remembrances organized for campaign photo-ops.

"The ouster of incumbents is considered *prima facie* proof of election irregularities, so everyone tends to vote for the incumbents to avoid the expense and displeasure of a runoff between the ousted incumbent and the rightful winner. If the rightful winner wins the runoff, which is difficult given the rampant ballot box stuffing and vote tampering, the incumbent files a Petition of Cancellation, and within fourteen business days, the rightful winner receives a Notice of Cancellation after which the Tetraminion Board of Elections is free to declare the incumbent or the rightful winner the winner, depending on which candidate has shown the proper gratitude."

17.
Orion

Twelve chimes ring out and the dark stirrings of dead memories rise in the quick of Polaris's runny eyes, hardening them to steel shafts which pin Bill to the wall like a science project bug. "And you are?" Polaris does not ask but demands of Bill.

"Bill Vine. And you?"

"Orion, a friend of Henry K.'s. Henry and Poly have been waiting for you for over an hour."

"The slippery dame lapped me. What a humbling day."

"Don't beat yourself up, Bill. A man doesn't stand a chance in these damn tunnels. Impossible to navigate without a map or a guide. I can't believe one of the Llumps didn't importune you for an escort fee. *Schlupping* devils know every inch of Tetraminion's catacombs, as they should. They were hired on to complete the risky work during the demolition phase. Did you know that all Llumps are experts in the handling of dynamite, plastic explosives and nitro glycerin, although there's not a single recorded instance of a Llump setting a charge that didn't prematurely detonate? So perhaps I'm thinking about washing dishes. Who can say? I'm not myself today, or any day for that matter. Come, Bill, there is much for us to discuss. But say nothing. As is sometimes the case, the more we say the less said, so the less said the more we say. I hold this true to my heart: the words of others always hold more value than our own, so take my advice and disregard everything I say. I find that works best, most of all for me."

71

18.
Bloodthirsty Cultists

The bustle of the complex is in the past now. A smoky gray memory to which Bill clings like a child as he and Orion stalk quietly through the turpitudes, lusts and false bereavements of bloodthirsty cultists. Dark figures in hooded vestments devour hunks of bloody meat from the limbs of a lean, hungry god of suffering. Suddenly, the hypnotic trill of satyr pipes filters up from the deepening distance, and the figures cease their ghoulish feast to hop in arrhythmic, spastic circles, like the unnatural, lifeless jerks of a marionette operated by a madman. Possessed hips gyrate in vile circles and hump the empty air, as arms loose as a rag doll's flail in uncoordinated lunges for a body, anybody, to embrace. Turgid members and wet clefts glide along sweat lathered skin without a hint of coupling or consummation or any act forbidden by sacred tomes handed down by the titular chieftains of a brutal age.

The continual distraction of ritual prevents the figures from tearing each other apart like savages and drinking the blood of the vanquished. Once in a while, they forget the lessons of civilization and start a long and terrible war in the name of their famished deity. Even as centuries of tireless chaos and death sweep across the land, the rituals proceed unimpeded, growing more and more elaborate to mask the din of war. Peacetime ensues and settles into a weary vacuum of even more ritual. Accumulated marble treasures and the pigments of master artisans idle away inside the vainglorious edifice of a city-state paved with riches.

Loss of purpose and identity leads to a period of loathsome, secret debauchery. Angels weep in beatified silence as bishops move pawns around the board in circles of shame. True believers lock themselves in chambers of denial. Do not enter, ye of burning truth!

Entrenchment protects the establishment from further damage, while the world grinds on an axis of festering wounds. An aging impotent figurehead issues apologia carried on broken dove wings turned to stone by the gaze of paper gorgons. In the wake of discredit, the rituals plod on with the deft intensity of apes flinging feces. Echoes of lapsed chants haunt empty pews. Elderly women with smudged foreheads and thin blue lips count backwards from the Omega to the Alpha, the end to the beginning, to dull the tumorous ache of cognitive dissonance. Repercussions shrink to blurbs and footnotes buried under an avalanche of misallocated sympathy. The pipes fade to a soft sigh of sound, indistinct as the silent screams of the unwept, and the hooded figures slip away in the night.

19.
Seeping

Damp gusts of stark realization shake brackish rainwater out of half-dead palm trees. Eyes swollen half-shut from bug bites, the taste of jungle rot and humid death are all Bill has to guide himself along the banks of a polluted river where blind fish with inward curving teeth leap for the shoreline, desperate to evolve legs and start a new life living off the co-opted land. The tortured squawks of extinct birds rattle through the jungle and infect the marrow of unwary travelers attuned to sympathy and justice and other counterculture nonsense. Bill is thankfully immune. "How much further is it?"

"Pretty far." Orion fires up two cigarettes, hands one to Bill. "You don't have to smoke it. Just wave it around like a sparkler. The leeches find the leafy aroma just as repellant as blood tainted with nicotine."

"Thanks," Bill pinches the cigarette between fingers fidgety with suppressed thoughts, the lapping heat of the coal rising and falling against his skin like the warm wet adulations of a childhood pet. "I apologize in advance for going ancient, but there's something I've got to get off my chest, something smaller than an albatross but bigger than a bread box. You don't mind, do you?" The steely gaze of Orion briefly flickers at Bill through thunderclouds of conjured smoke. "I'll take your silence for affirmation. Anyways, when I was six going on seven, my mother came down with a case of benway. The only way to contract it is from the bite of a mosquito native to tropical climates. The doctor, an aging quack, told her the larva must've hitched a ride in a crate of pomegranates, as if she gave a damn about the pedigree of her exotic condition. There are no medicinal curatives for benway, so he prescribed an intense series of hot water immersion treatments. Seeping he called it, claiming it would clear up her condition in record time. We were dirt poor and couldn't afford the luxury of hydro therapy, so the doc arranged to treat her *pro bono* on an outpatient basis. Unusual for a doctor to resort to legal jargon, but not unprecedented.

"During the first week of seeping, besides a chronic case of wrinkled fingers and toes, there was a marked improvement in her condition. The fever dissipated and there was a clarity to her eyes that had been missing since the Gilded Age. But the price of that clarity was a troubled mind, for five times in as many days, she bore witness to the total dissolution of a human being. People as solid as you and I were dissolving in hot mineral water like cubes of chicken bouillon. Nothing left but a pair of earrings or a wristwatch corroding at the bottom of a tub."

20.

Anxiety

"She wanted to confess everything to the doc, but couldn't bring herself to do it. The implications regarding her sanity, or the lack thereof, were too obvious. So with no other viable alternatives, she resolved to bottle up her anxiety. In six hours, she filled a gallon jug to the brim with pure, uncut anxiety. By the end of the treatments, our apartment was an anxiety warehouse. Bottle after bottle lined the baseboards in neat grocery-store pyramids. We even had to lease space at a storage facility. My father, a bookkeeper for a small Midwest department store chain, blew his top and demanded the disposal of the surplus anxiety before the storage costs bankrupted the family. She agreed that it'd become a problem and invited the neighbors over for a sample. They instantly fell in love with my mother's anxiety and bought seven bottles.

"Before long, every flat in the complex was hungry for a taste of my mother's anxiety. They staged anxiety mixers that dragged on for days and days. Dedicated professionals skipped work to stay ripped to the gills on paralyzing quantities of undiluted anxiety. Budding careers were ruined, happy marriages destroyed. Children traumatized for life. Disgruntled customers tried suing us for fraud, negligence, breach of contract, but nothing held up in court. The authorities were aching to bust us, too. Detectives spent days combing the penal code for any legal obscurantism we might be in violation of. They couldn't find squat. We paid our taxes on time. Didn't violate any health codes. Put *extra* change in the parking meters. If we saw a piece of trash on the sidewalk, we picked it up and threw it away in the nearest receptacle. Model citizens, through and through. Yet the fuzz was still frothing mad that we were raking in so much dough for something unproductive as distributing anxiety. All the same, when it became clear that the cops wouldn't relent, my father made a generous donation to the policemen's benevolence fund, and the heat lifted. My father didn't get upset at the hypocrisy inherent in this transaction. He chalked it up to the nature of things. People get ticked at the random fortunes of others. There's a reason they call them windfall profits: they happen at the whim of the wind. And who should profit from the weather besides weathermen and umbrella salesmen?"

21.
Nightmarish Tableaus

"The gravy train hit the end of the line when my mother stopped feeling anxious. My father tried everything imaginable to get her to fret. He levied death threats, entertained pushing her in front of a moving bus. Alluded to defenestration during every dinner table discussion. Nothing worked. Then the economy took a turn for the worse and my father got laid off, and the anxiety tit started flowing again, regular as milk in Bessie, but none of the new batch was saleable. The quality of her anxiety dropped precipitously once it was no longer connected to a fear of institutionalization. What little we'd saved from the heydays of the anxiety operation my father invested in a second regimen of seeping treatments, a move my mother categorically rejected. She had no interest in reenacting her steady creep toward the edge of insanity. Still, the mere implication of returning to the clinic produced the desired effect. Her anxiety returned to its former potency. But the bottom had fallen out of the market. Supply so outpaced demand that you couldn't give away a gallon of high grade anxiety unless it came with a penthouse apartment.

"My father, a pragmatist to the bitter end, went to the doctor with some cockamamie story about contracting parasitic dysentery from a bale of Egyptian cotton and took the treatments himself. It was his peculiar way of assuring us he'd found a way to repurpose the squandered nest egg. It only took him three days of seeping to start seeing people dissolve. Father didn't possess a constitution capable of distilling anxiety. He instead painted nightmarish tableaus. Every one of them centered on the same mad theme of water as a kind of human solvent. To be a recreational swimmer, high diver, surfboarder, lifeguard, scuba diver or bathing beauty in one of his paintings was a fatal mistake. His technique gave the impression that the people were candles melting on a radiator. Victims of circumstance. That they dissipated to nothing was just the lot they had drawn in life, or the lot drawn for them, or the lot they had been drawn to reflect. The difference among the three interpretations is immaterial.

"A prestigious gallery owned by a renowned connoisseur of modern art fell head-over-heels in love with my father's macabre body of work. He staged a coming out party for the Vine Collection and invited critics from every major news outlet to review the brightest sensation to hit the art world since Renaldo Clemmons. The show went over like a Nazi revival in a synagogue, a heinous flop so damaging to the gallery's reputation the owner was laughed out of the business, ostracized from the world of art, reduced to rubble.

"In a word, ruined."

22.
The Thing That Slept Under Bill's Bed

"The fat ones are hungry today." Orion shivers his back and a mantle of leeches falls into the black, soupy mystery of the swamp. He fires up a second cigarette and bellows the cherry to a fiendish red. Gray curtains of smoke sift through the moldering jungle canopy. The feint sound of war drums vibrates hidden life from the trees. Hushed scurries of wide-eyed lemurs. Clambering hiss of lean, nimble pumas. Sluggish slither of mottled boas fat with half-digested pygmies. To keep the peckish leeches at bay, Bill and Orion fashion a crude raft out of uprooted bamboo trees and red and white striped vines. Floating atop the water, however, isn't much safer than wading through it. Orion and Bill are swarmed from all sides by hucktoads, mawkish amphibians drawn to makeshift watercraft traveling under allegorical circumstances. "This man your father destroyed," Orion pauses to swat a sortie of hucktoads back into the drink, "does he have a name?"

"Every man does. It's just I cannot bring myself to say it aloud. He is the Thing That Slept under My Bed as a child. A nameless menace. I can still see his hard, pale lips, the lips of a cadaver, quivering over the body of my father. He didn't mean to do it. It was an impulsive, unconscious act. He had small, powerful hands with a mind of their own. The precocious hands did all the dirty work. Picked up the car keys, unlocked the car, started it up, piloted the vehicle the six miles to our impoverished neck of the woods, opened the front door to our unit, guided him up the handrail, steadied his hesitant steps and barged inside our flat. The hands shoved aside my mother and wrapped themselves around the throat of my father until they'd strangled the life out of the unemployed bookkeeper who'd painted rubbish and ruined their bewildered custodian. The police took the hands into custody, separate from the art connoisseur, by sawing the murderous instruments off at the wrist. Things got ugly when the hands turned state's evidence and ratted out the art connoisseur as the responsible party. Judge Okley declared a mistrial and sentenced the involved parties to indefinite incarceration until the courts could sort out the immigration status of the hands. Severed body parts don't retain the citizenship status of the person to which they were formally attached. The judge considered deporting the hands, but a set of mitigating circumstance netted the hands leniency.

"The department store that'd laid off the late Danny Vine had taken out a life insurance contract to indemnify itself against his premature demise. Standard procedure for all peasants under its employ. A clerical error listed his contract as current, so the department store unwittingly continued to pay the premiums. But as Danny Vine was an *ex*-employee, they were disqualified as beneficiaries. However, as blood relatives my mother and I were entitled to collect under the double indemnity clause for a murder, provided a potential beneficiary didn't commit the murder. Determined to escape the disgrace of paying on a contract, the insurance company marshaled its resources to frame my mother for the murder and struck the art connoisseur from the court records as thoroughly as Moses' name from Egypt, assuming we buy the Bible's version of the events. They would've gotten away with it if not for overlooking the villainous hands, which, having claimed to see the err of their ways, agreed to exonerate my mother by confessing to the *involuntary* murder of Danny Vine in exchange for time served.

"It was all an act, obviously, to any chump with peepers

and a scorecard. Within a month, the famous *artiste* the Great Donasso, rendered handless by a maverick chain saw during a wood carving demo, accepted the cold, calculating demons as grafts. My mother wrote a series of letters to the Great Donasso warning him not to trust the devilish hands, elaborating the donor organs' reputation for wickedness. All of them were returned unopened, the envelopes soiled with black fingerprints arrayed in a manner that projected an air of utter contempt for her meddling."

23.
Dishonest Solution

"Two years passed as years tend to, quickly, and my mother opened the newspaper to a story about the showing of a new art collection by the Great Donasso, and in the center of the page was a photograph of a painting that was the spit-and-image of a painting hanging in our home, one of my father's catastrophic failures at the art game. In fact, every painting in the show was a plagiarized copy of my father's work. The show got rave reviews. Talk of the town. The rip-offs were sold on the spot for five to six figures a pop. My mother contacted the gallery owner and laid on a cock-and-bull story about a Grant Wood painting that'd been in the family for two generations, could he please come out and hang a price on it. Within the hour, a dandy in some exorbitant French threads knocked on our door. Real detached asshole, his whole body puckered with contempt for his surroundings. We invited him in, and the bastard didn't get two steps inside the joint before he's accosted by a dozen paintings sold not a day ago to well-heeled sophisticates as originals. All he could manage were the pitiable grunts of an old man passing a kidney stone. The dandy was so overwrought with grief he collapsed on our secondhand sofa like a de-boned fish. In his helpless state, we laid the whole tale on him, stem to stern, the evil hands, where they were now and so on. When the dandy regained his composure, he proposed a mutually beneficial solution and offered to buy the originals with the intent to destroy them. We negotiated a fair price, a wire transfer for half the gross, and he strolled out with the damning evidence bound for the nearest incinerator. Happy ending, right?

"Not for the devious hands. They mistook us for do-gooders, seekers of justice and truth. But justice and truth, noble ends unto themselves, don't fill your belly. In an orgy of insanity, the hands squandered the Great Donasso's fortune on loose women, auction house wines, prescription meds and collectible plush toys before spontaneously amputating and pushing the Great Donasso off a balcony to his death, which was ruled a misadventure. The hands then began to stalk us, hungry to avenge what they perceived on our part as a moral failing. Around the corner from our flat, we found whole cigarettes unsullied but for some scorch marks at the tip. The hands had a mean smoking habit but lacked the lungs necessary to inhale. There was a steady stream of notes stuffed under our door, each an overture announcing our imminent strangulation. Crank calls woke us in the wee hours of the night. We reported the incidents and went before Judge Oberog, who informed us the disembodied hands had secured a restraining order against *us*, and if we violated it, he'd send us both up the river for deuce, prison for my mother, reform school for me.

"My mother spent some of the hush money on a private dick with a malleable set of morals and bills to pay. The PI tailed the hands to a Z Street flophouse where he observed the subject shooting junk into its stumps and manipulating male privates for a couple of bucks a feel. Stupid hands had the world by the balls and threw it all away to fondle balls in smaller, more personal increments. The PI dropped an anon tip to the cops. The hands were busted for possession of narcotics and solicitation. A meatball judge with a soft spot for the plight of junkies and prostitutes set the bail so low it was as if he were daring the hands to jump bail, which they did, jumped and disappeared into the dark folds of the city's underbelly."

24.
Iterations of Paranoia

"Months of scrabbling friendless and alone in the shivering night splintered the nails and shrank the skin to a brittle, anemic crust. Malnourishment had finally caught up with the fugitive hands, too many days of roughing it without a circulatory system with which to rejuvenate the tissues. Ostracized from the loosely knit encampments of panhandlers and vagabonds and strays of the land, the hands lit out for the country to start a new life, hoping to hook up with a farmer who'd lost his instruments of the harvest in a combine accident, a common injury among men in that lionized profession.

"Lost in a field of corn stubble, the hands, barely able to crawl after fending off a pack of wild dogs, made it to the mouth of a stable, where a farmer's wife found them lying in scribbles of hay, broken, beaten, shriveled and near death. She took pity on the hands and milked her veins, transfused her essence into the corrupt tissues, and reawakened the evil within. The hands went on a rural killing spree. Whole families strangled to death in their beds. Bull-necked truck drivers, strangled behind the wheel, plowed into pit stops, gift shops, ran through live gas pumps. Explosions rocked the foundations of homesteads at the crumbling edges of society. Greasy black smoke painted the sky in weepy dribs and drabs. The governor declared martial law. National guardsmen roamed the streets arresting anyone out past curfew. Families were snatched from backyard barbeques and frogmarched whimpering into the black mouth of unmarked state-owned cages on wheels where hooded figures conducted brutal interrogations that took days, sometimes weeks to finish.

"Nobody was above suspicion, not even my mother and I, who had cooperated every step of the way. They kidnapped us, too, rode us around the block fifty or sixty times, screaming and blaring boat-horns two inches from our ears. We wailed, spat and pissed ourselves in terror while a second squad of peacekeepers turned our home inside-out. What did they think we were hiding from the authorities? Nothing. It was a mix-up. The target was our neighbors, one flat over. Same first number. Similar last number. 'Mistakes have been made,' the chief investigator told the small huddled clot of cowed specters comprising the state-approved press corps. They scribbled words on scraps of paper then handed them to a large captain in combat fatigues, who disposed of the paper down the throat of a metal shaft that plummeted to the HQ of an incineration operation which ran twenty-four-seven. 'Ashes never betray secrets,' was their unofficial motto. Unofficial because the edict approving it had been incinerated. Media personalities sat stiffly behind burning desks reading scripts approved by the state, eyes fixed on the lens, the gleam of off-camera muzzles squared to sweaty temples twinkling in the corners of turgid, terrified stares. 'There is nothing to fear,' the words escaped the news anchor's painted smile in quivering slobbers. 'The government is in complete control of the situation. Demonstrations of unquestionable cooperation are the highest form of patriot—' The broadcast ended with the ubiquitous hands choking the life out of her. There was an honest hatred full of passion behind the strangulation, as if you were witness the evening of a score with an ex-lover who'd scorned the rekindling of an old affair.

"Lost in a fogbound panic, the state outlawed privacy. Pissing or shitting behind closed doors was punishable by forced surgical implantation of a catheter or colostomy bag. Everyone had to sleep elbow to elbow like living sardines. Sleeping without the implicit supervision of a partner was considered a confession of wrongdoing. Lie detectors were installed throughout the state's crumbling infrastructure, inside sinkholes in the asphalt and under slabs of concrete upheaved from countless cruel winters. Sirens blared when someone in the vicinity of the polygraph sensors told a lie, however innocuous, even civilized, it may be. Nobody bothered to calibrate the machines to differentiate lies under oath or to the authorities from harmless utilitarian fibs, nominal boasts and minor sidesteppings of the truth to soften the blow to a friend's ego. Night and day, the tempestuous screams of sirens betrayed the location of the newest fibber for the police to arrest on suspicion of collaborating with an enemy of the state. Once in a while, the hands killed a random citizen to work the panic up to a fine froth. Within months, cameras blanketed the state, and the watchers watched us and each other, and we watched them watching us and each other, and they in turn watched us watching them watching us and each other and so on in endless iterations of paranoia that to this very day continue to sap the coffers of the state. The state long ago convinced itself that the only way to secure its long term survival was to commit suicide as slowly as possible."

25.
Orion's Poem

When it's clear that Bill has finished, Orion wets his lips, now gleaming with spittle, and recites a poem:

> "Thunder at the mountain gate,
> Has smitten us to sundered dust,
> Rendered us to bitter hate,
> Reshaped our ageless wanderlust
> To shrouds and tears and stiffened state."

Bill chuckles, not in mockery but in self-derision. "What I said, but in far fewer words. Who's it by?"

"Nobody. I read it on a bathroom wall somewhere. Really makes you think, doesn't it?"

26.

Renaissance

The red and white vines release their stranglehold on the bamboo shafts and slither into the water. The deck of the raft drifts apart, forms a crisscross of malevolent I-Ching hexagrams and then sinks into the muted turmoil of shallow muck centuries in the making. Orion and Bill wade toward the closest riverbank, where the shoreline is choked with disturbed cairns marking the graves of men who died on the field of some battle for something somewhere down the foggy trails of the past. Nameless round stones stare up at the sky with blank intensity as one-legged frogs hop in circles to taunt snakes feasting on their own tails. Mangy bobcats drag helpless hares up to the rafters of tall, unclassifiable trees. Gore-soaked muzzles gnaw, gnash and tear through flesh and bone. The earth and roots below are baptized in dribbles of warm blood and saliva. Gorged on meat and blood, the sated bobcats push the hare carcasses out of the trees and watch the bodies crash through bare branches then twirl out of control like a broken toy unleashed from the trembling fists of a hyperactive child. Bodies and earth reunite with a distant finality that captures the imaginations of the bobcats for a brief moment that is instantly wiped from memory. The bobcats climb down from the upper reaches to sink their hot fangs in the next generation of hares caught unawares at the dawning of a New Age of enlightenment. The Old Age steps on the heels of the New, as a warning that it is not in any way special or exceptional. Two steps forward, a hundred steps back. Repeat the pattern; call it a Renaissance and sell, sell, sell!

27.
Henry's Remarks

The disarray of the broken cairns ends at the shiny pink mouth of a giant clamshell amphitheater with a state of the art PA system and seating for up to two thousand people, or seven thousand Llumps if you remove the seats. The venue has been leased by Henry K. on behalf of the Negáshun Biannual Symposium on Hygiene for Llumps, Llumpattoes and Other Social Cancers Our Sacred Body Politic Has Yet to Remit. The event is a sellout, and a sellout. But who's to judge that which we, *by definition*, have an obligation to judge? Henry stands at the podium, preparing to make the opening remarks. His shoulders droop at the prospect of how few audience members, degenerates one and all, will appreciate his clever insights, ironic asides and superior taste in apparel.

"Wenches and scallywags, scumbags, cumbags, and undesirables of all ages: cleanliness, as you *feelthy* subtypes of our fast-deteriorating society may or may not be aware of, is adjacent to ghastliness." Henry repositions the mike closer to his lips so the intense odor of his bad intentions infects the PA monitors and saturates the unwary spectators in his inner, unprocessed rot. "That is the best any of you can hope for, given your inherent genetic limitations. While it's natural to resent the higher born, who shall always be regarded as cleaner than you are, if for no other reason than what some so-called experts in the field of racial taxonomy call 'indisputable truth,' I urge you all to fight the temptation to further alienate yourselves by erecting cultural barriers, such as peculiar dialects and hair styles, and musical subcultures

90

bound to advance the acceptance of broad, albeit accurate, stereotypes.

"Try your best to blend in as seamlessly as possible by subordinating your devolved tastes to preconceived cultural norms designed to gentrify your individuality. What some of you mistake for creativity and self-expression, the province of artists (if you have to ask what qualifies someone as an artist, then you don't know what one is), presents additional obstacles toward your eventual absorption by the System, which is paramount if any of you rejects expect to get ahead in life. Scrubbing behind the ears, where applicable, does not qualify as a passport to success. You must scrub your entire worldview to reflect the shiny, pink hue of health all of you lack externally."

The deep rumbles of war roll through the crowd.

"Now, now, settle down. I'm not equipped to drain this many simpering blobs of pus at once. What I mean to say is that it is not the System which has to change but you who must let the System change your perceptions of what you think you are. Once integrated into the System, the concrete reality of your existential selves is of no consequence. It is often taken for granted that the System's transformative powers extend to those inside the System. Nonsense. The System exists to serve the System, as do you. If you do not serve the System, then the System has no use for you. So it is imperative that you consciously make yourselves useful to the System or the System will *find* a use for you, one that I guarantee none of you shall deem as uplifting."

28.
Diary of a Mad Poet

Unruly audience members rise in concert from the cold cement to hurl rotten vegetables at Henry, whose ducking skills are unparalleled. He's limber as an acrobat, plus he has the added handicap of a target on his chest to ensure that his performance is well received. A muscle-bound Ecund security guard with kitten-thick sideburns and a habit of chewing on toothpicks wades out into the crowd, bumping aside spectators like stubborn cattle. A boy enamored of the uniform lightly runs his fingers over the stripes on the Ecund's blue sleeve. The Ecund smiles grimly at the boy. Just the excuse he's been aching for. A piece of black bloodied wood, primitive yet elegant, makes a sudden appearance in hand. It is no ordinary armory-issued weapon, but a wondrous musical instrument through which the Ecund conducts a symphony of violence.

"This one's for you, and for you, and for you!" the Ecund cries in time with the meaty blows, the toothpick hopping with glee as he smashes in the face of a Llump washer woman, the pulped brain matter and bone reconfigured to a grotesque smile of admiration. The song rises and falls, the notes crisp and concise as the runny slush of pulverized skulls congeals at his feet. A red silence falls over the pavilion, the audience soaking up the brutal brilliance of his performance which so eclipses Henry's ducking routine the snobbish hack who writes the *Tetraminion Times* arts and entertainment section won't even trouble to pen a review. A glimmer of comprehension lights up the Ecund's waxy blue cheeks, now ruddy with ecstatic awareness. The toothpick shivers like a virgin bride at the thought of the carnage to come, the knurled fist withdrawing a Ugandan semi-automatic of an obscene, unheard of caliber. Big Bertha he calls it, coos to it, the steadying hand stroking the barrel with pornographic bliss as six-foot flames spew from the powder-blackened muzzle scorching the tips of his fingers a painfully vibrant pink. The bodies, piled three feet high, ooze vital fluids to the point where the cement is slippery as an amusement park slide. The Ecund, paying more attention to his toothpick than the footing, slips and falls and feigns unconsciousness from a minor head wound.

"We've got a man down!" yells the Ecund's partner who radios HQ. The Ecund captain intercepts the call, stroking his hair with long, delicate fingers as a Llump seamstress fits him for a slinky sequined ball gown. "Send the paramedics!" the captain screams spitting mad into a plastic Princess telephone plugged into a baboon's anus. The baboon translates the vibrations transmitted to his colon and forwards a memo scrawled in baboon to a nervous, cross-eyed desk sergeant who hasn't taken a decent crap in ten years. The sergeant's watery, unfocused eyes misinterpret the message, and he dispatches Ecund shock-troops equipped with an assortment of unethical tactical weapons banned by the Vargas Conventions: a dozen old clammy ketchup gas shells from the Great Condiment Conflict of '57, a canister of Queue Virus (the infected stand in line at the grocery store to buy one can of condensed soup, head home and then repeat the process until they run out of money or cabinet space), a box of shotgun shells filled with heavy confetti (slightly eradiated isotope variant of regular confetti arising from broken New Year's resolutions; see Blue Monday), and a vial of pretense drained from the diary of a mad poet. Spill one drop of the vial's purple jelly and the arteries of the earth harden. Plate tectonics cease. All motion freezes at the molecular level. The planet exudes one final groan of agony then heaves listlessly in the firmament, shudders and spins into the sun. A burning white flash in the corona as the atmosphere is consumed by fire. The blast melts the earth to a clinker that winks out of existence.

Before giving the order to deploy, the sergeant accidentally empties the vial into his coffee, drinks it, and takes a long smooth crap.

The best in all his life.

29.
Rebellion

Wounded Llumps and Llumpattoes *schlup* and scramble for the exits in a churning panic of blood and fear. The shock troop sirens sing to them in the distance of the bloodbath soon to come. A strapping Llump with bulging pseudopods calms the crowd with a gentle brush of his powerful charisma. He is a leader among leaders. The One who promises to bring the Llumps out of the darkness of repression. The shock troops arrive on the scene louder than a thunderclap in hell. Big men in jet black helmets and broad leather belts, armed with shotguns, rifles, shields, battering rams and hoses that spew liquid fire. They march on the crowd, prepared to send everyone to an early grave as soon as an early dinner. The One confronts the Ecunds by himself. Crazy fool or prophet, it doesn't matter; he gains the instant respect of the Ecunds to whom strength is everything. Nervous tension builds to a head. An errant shot rings out. The One falls and Tetraminion falls silent for a minute before falling into utter chaos and intractable rebellion.

Continuous fires submerge neighborhoods and business districts in thick black bands of smoke. The horizon glows with the orangey apathy of a half-spent jack-o-lantern. The air is yellow and sulfurous. Ecunds, looters and other undesirable elements captured by the rebels dance in the trees like wind chimes. Under the dangling bodies, women place steel pails to catch cold dribbles of sperm ejaculated at the moment of death while men torch fields of saw grass. Fingers of fire caress the earth like a deadly lover as rebel quarry crouching in the fields suddenly pop up like corn kernels jumping in hot oil. But it's too late. The speeding flames soak everything up in a mop of heat and smoke. The fires go out, leaving blackened plains and condemned scarecrows of bones. "Victory is ours!" the rebels cry through teeth broken off at the gum line from premature celebrations. Small boys pick through the ashes and load charred skulls onto large metal carts driven by teams of wild horses. Wild dogs dig their snouts into the smoldering pelvises and report their findings to assertiveness trainers. "That one's somewhat downbeat, overcooked even. But nothin' a dose of confidence and a thorough leg humpin' can't cure."

Ecund forces rout the rebels in the downtown business district, headquarters to the System. The losses are great, but the gains, in the blinkered eyes of the sheep taught to bleat at grotesque demonstrations of power, are greater. The battlefront bulges and spills into living rooms. Explosions knock the sleeping public from soft beds of complacency. Corpses bearing shocked expressions of wonderment, those unaware there was a war in progress, are heaped on toy wagons and taken to funeral pyres which burn day and night to keep spirits of the kill at bay. Old men with milky blue eyes transcribe the virtues of pacifism to parchments stashed in beatnik hangouts, for future generations to study and flout, and transcribe yet again.

The rebels fall back to the outermost rim of Tetraminion, the landfill zone, where gargantuan garbage volcanoes wreathed in clouds of grit and grime vomit filth from slobbering cones. Here, they will make their final stand against the forces of darkness. The oldest story ever resold and repackaged a million times. The ground is soft and spongy as a baby blanket but deadly as a minefield. The heavy Ecund shock troops sink into the mire and bray like brainless donkeys. Llump commandos trained in the dark arts of shadow *schlupping* and pseudopod-jitsu break over the bogged down Ecunds in howling tidal waves of meat, bashing, crushing and annihilating every living thing in their path. The rebel commander, a dashing Llump with broad shoulders and a constant three-day growth of whiskers, plants a flagpole in the chasse of a television shaggy with colonies of exotic moss cultured to thrive in the castoff lunacy of a vanishing death cult. Stout pseudopods work the lanyard until a broad banner of unconscious desires and untamable ambitions unfurls in the morning sun for the pried open eyes of the dead and dying Ecunds to behold.

30.
Cantina

The rebellion recruits Henry and Orion as spin doctors, while Bill and Poly make the nut as commissioned officers in the Languor Brigade, special forces trained to spread self-doubt throughout the enemy ranks, and the ranks of the rebellion if Bill has any say in the matter. For desertion in face of nothing particularly menacing, the rebel commander, as counseled by Henry, sentences Bill and Poly to lounge detail in the dismal cantina located on the lower decks of the Transport. The house specialty is third-tier snake oil served in mugs misty with condescension. Outmoded televisions broadcast updates received from the future. All of them sputter and hiss dead air.

"What a dump," Poly licks dribbles of snake oil from the rim of her glass then flaps her tongue down the shaft of the mug, practicing her technique for a later encounter with the commander, "makes me long for a case of infected piles."

The bartender, a florid surf guitar aficionado, Acapulco shirt tucked into Chinos two sizes too big for his emaciated frame, stands in buckets of flat soapsuds hocking spit on mugs that he has no intention of polishing. "I wouldn't be levying criticism, skank. Your role as a customer in a place this low casts extreme doubts on your character. I, on the other hand, am beyond reproach, since I'm a victim of inadequate secondary training programs and must lower myself to crawling in the muck to make the ends before I can begin to worry about arranging their rendezvous."

"Ever notice, Bill, how philosophical degrees always seem to accompany mixologist degrees."

Employing his Languor Brigade training, Bill feigns interest in the subject at hand and stares wistfully into space, riveted but in a bored sort of way. "Nope."

"Me neither."

A gang of Llump commandoes bangs into the cantina. All of them are abnormal by even *feelthy* Llump standards, smaller and less cohesive than the typical Llump, with skin dull and rough as unrefined coal; lean, muscular pseudopods that project a protected inner fragility; and eyes which float aimlessly in rolling swells of tissue, eyes haunted and cruel and alight with the guarded sheen of ghouls pawing through open graves. The largest commando *schlups* behind the bar (an old time maneuver stolen from any given oater) and helps himself to a bottle of snake oil. Loud, rambunctious whoops of approval drown out the hissing TVs. The milky whites of the bartender's eyes fill with strangled fear. He stares down into the soapsuds, studying the thin white film on the surface for an exit strategy, any way to extricate himself from an insolvable predicament.

The Llump shimmies up a stool, climbs on the bar and starts to sing in a foreign tongue evocative of a drowning victim's last gurgles, a watery, fatal dirge that explodes against the eardrums in sprays of brackish fear tainted with the taste of high-tide coral fragments and choking ropes of kelp. Then a guttural mantra strikes up, every Llump chanting at first in a low, raspy moan that builds to rumbling roars of sublime sorrow. Unconsummated dreams and lost loves rise up out of the fog of song and linger before the barkeep, who begins to weep uncontrollably. What has he done with his life? Is this all he is, a lowly servant? What became of that fine young man with his vaunted aspirations? Reduced to dust and monsters and the torments of jocund spirits.

The chant ends. The final note a sweet parting. A plunge toward voided destiny.

The Llump draws a long curving onyx blade, recites an ancient prayer and begins the rite of *gringeification*, ritualistic suicide in which the Llump stabs himself in the guts and churns the blade with such rapidity his being liquefies to *gringe*. The bartender yelps and flees the cantina, trailing clouds of unspoken cruelties and prejudices as the commandoes honor their fallen comrade by taking him into their bodies to live forever as an agent of cyclical wretchedness preparing for a dark harvest, each generation devouring its predecessors, compounding the sins of fathers and sons down through the howling, pitiless ages.

When the last blob of *gringe* has been gobbled, the commandoes fold with the shadows to petition murderous pagan gods for the clemency of deserted hope laid naked before the fall of the headsman's axe.

31.
Zombie Programming

One of the dead TVs comes suddenly to life. Zombie programming. Rotten teeth and gray skin lurch at the screen to gorge on the suffocated, zip-locked thoughts of mesmerized viewers. Image of a large, bloated aircraft soaring through cotton candy clouds. Target acquired, the bomb bay doors open like an autopsy scar, and the humming behemoth drops its payload. The bombardier snaps pictures of the run from ten thousand feet up. He gets a nice one of the impact, a single dot of white light no bigger than a remnant from a paper punch. The motivations behind the bombing run are redacted and re-redacted until every significant document connected to the mission is a black hole pregnant with destroyed information. Historians study the negative energy contained in those pages like the Dead Sea Scrolls. Theories arise as to what they once said, all of them wrong, none of them shorter than a Proust novel.

Reams and reams of paper wasted to describe wasted paper.

One volume, preserved in Haiti, is so massive it takes up half of the country. People live on the book, make their homes on it, fucking and cooking and fighting on the pages. Haitian children lay on their bellies reading and staining the pages with curious fingers, trying to make sense of any of it. What is the meaning of this? they wonder and ask their parents, who ask other parents who ask other people from other parts of the world, none of them positive who asked the question which triggered the global circle jerk. Roll credits over a medium shot of the zombie gnawing off its own arm caught in endlessly looping reruns.

The broadcast day comes to a close. Cue the Negáshun national anthem, "That Ol' Gang of Mine," playing while a montage of unconvincing pastoral stills vomits sappy, gangrenous nostalgia into unconscious living rooms. After that comes a test pattern which stamps its image on a generation, a decapitated Indian head decked in full ceremonial headdress over a target. Sly symbolism too heady for the average Puritan to ken, yet it kindles a kind of primitive ecstasy for the suffering of inferiors. Tinny speakers shriek a note held forever transmitted into space as proof of sentient life in this desolate sector of the universe.

Bill and Poly drain their glasses and fall asleep in each other's arms like spent lovers camped under a canopy of stars. Nightmarish constellations wheel in the night sky on broken axles. Nowhere to run or hide. This planet, our inheritance, is all there is. Predawn dew clings to the open faces of trembling leaves rapturous with birdsong.

32.
A New System

Come daybreak, gods will be conjured up from memory then slaughtered on alters of burning rubbish. Scales tip one way then the other. Nothing is gained; everything is lost, fractured. Citizens on both sides of the conflict experience total mental collapse. Personalities splinter and shard. Epic battles staged on drawing room sofas involve prominent businessmen flailing and flagellating themselves with strips of glass-encrusted leather. Hunks of bloody back meat cake fine upholstery and outstanding furnishings. The businessmen insist their side is winning, even as the moon ripens to a bloody pimple prepared to pop at any moment. Amphibian rains pelt rooftops, collapsing the market for frog's legs and crippling gourmet restaurants. Greenish smog wanders the streets slaying first born Llumps, collapsing the *gringe* market and crippling the System. In response, Negáshun's President, a stuffed beaver bolted to a log, deploys national guardsmen to gun down college campus protestors, then waits quietly by the red phone for a call from a dead hillbilly in a sequined jumpsuit.

The tatty silhouettes of Bill and Poly slog up a smoldering hillock to bask in the echoes of bygone life haunting the charred jagged wreckage of Tetraminion. Emergency radios turned to maximum volume shout static at one another. Bed sheets snagged on crisped branches snap in the driving winds with the dry persistence of whipsong. Stagnant convocations flutter by distorted regurgitations of depraved faith. Trudging through the smoke and steam, teams of Llumps harnessed to great sheering devices scissor the foundations of madness in twain.

A welcome sign of *pro*gress.

Harrows churn and plow under the skeletal remains of the past and plant the seeds of tomorrow, which sprout overnight into a verdant beggars' paradise. Phosphorescent immigrants flock to the rejuvenated lands of Negáshun, bright, cheerful folk bloated to the gills with the grim, wishful thoughts of holocaust survivors trying to forget the unforgettable. The backbone of *pro*gress arches like a frightened feline, a nimble creature that always lands on its feet, and tiptoes furtively toward new foundations of commerce. A new System, much the same as the old System, arrives with a warm smile and an open hand, a twinkle in the eye. All part of the ritual, of course, to sweeten the kill. Get in close, close enough to get a good strong whiff of good intentions, then, while our backs are turned, the beast within rises, a towering, slavering, ineffable giant of immortal bearing summoned from nowhere by no one whose countenance provokes terror such as the heart and mind has never imagined, yet the soul, that crafty inner intangible, sees it for what it is, our collective misery made flesh by the willful ignorance and immeasurable avarice of men.

33.
Permanent Records

Come nightfall, Negáshun slips back into its smothering routines of social stratification, segregation, intolerance and economic strife. Llump laborers, persuaded by quixotic tales of the impossible, toil night and day for pennies, hoping golden shower trickles will burst forth from clear blue skies. Seekers and visionaries wait in three-day-long lines for payday advances due yesterday. Cheap financing, easy terms, customers pledge all their future potential earnings in exchange for the carnival mirror illusion of financial security. Pointy-voiced spinsters berate children from pulpits of standardized venom. Suspected dreamers are torn forcibly from their mother's arms and fed into the gears of the System for refurbishing. Blinkers are riveted into raw infant bone, the tiny eyelids peeled back like the skin of a grape. Any wrinkles of individuality are flattened out and mainstreamed to a jaundiced, putrid outlook, all unapproved aspirations raped, gutted and tossed to the bottom of a well. Fiends wrapped in moldering folkways stamp up and down school halls barking slogans written to sell luxury automobiles, cigarettes and beer. Since failure is predetermined at birth, the teachers grade nothing and file everything in anonymous steel cabinets at the Hall of Permanent Records, notorious for its horrendous recordkeeping.

Guidance counselors groom the economically disadvantaged for fulfilling careers as spiritual assassins. Black clouds of defeat follow them like stray animals, raining buckets of ridicule and doubt on the dreams and aspirations of coworkers, underlings and hapless strangers.

Ego-crushing blows dealt to friends and family members on the verge of making it big yield giant bonuses deposited in the karmic ruins of studio apartment overdoses. The lucky ones train as fortune tellers reading chicken guts, tea leaves and overactive sweat glands for ten ciphers a pop. "So sad to inform you that everything you suspect about the future shall come to pass, and all of it far worse than you imagined." The ability to emphasize the futility of life in disheartening detail finally pays off in the end when a dissatisfied customer pulls a Lugar and squeezes off six rounds pointblank into a rented crystal ball. Shards of glass foggy with false prognostications and phony portents explode through the air in unpredictable patterns, killing an obnoxious pop star with a deep-seated fear of waiting rooms.

The shoddy patchwork of New Tetraminion radiates an impervious animosity forever simmering inside a shell of sour misgivings. Unreconciled grievances express themselves as random acts of senseless but economically stimulative violence. Entire Llump families are found pureed in their beds, the raw *gringe* bagged as evidence forwarded for processing, and sometimes in transit to the plant the confiscated *gringe* mysteriously disappears, the evidence bags immaculate of any signs of *gringe* but for gooey smears of saliva and, occasionally, traces of pseudopod slime.

Destitution filling its belly on the scrapings of destitution.

34.
Henry's Testimonial

"The seriousness of this sudden outburst of cannibalism cannot be understated," Henry testifies before the House Committee on Unimportant Affairs. The diamond studding his tie clasp winks affectionately to the flashing cameras. Call girls wrapped in mink stoles head under the Committee table to deliver a little bit of the same. "While it is imperative to save the Llumpulation from itself, it is also important not to undermine the role of natural selection in thinning unpopular sectors of the public. Dodo birds weren't eradicated by hunters. They were eradicated by a congenital inability to adapt to the hunters' desire to hunt them. If the Llumps cannot find the will to refrain from eating each other, then I say to blazes with them. Nurse! Prep a patient, any patient at all. Sick, well, it doesn't matter. I must illustrate my meaning for the benefit of these overstuffed Philistines…that is to say, fine stewards of governance."

A team of Llump nurses (most of them male Llumps in drag) *schlups* into the chamber wheeling a sickly pale boy— the spit-and-image of Bill Vine—strapped to a steel gurney. The boy's so clammy with feverish death you can taste on his sour breath the effluence of the putrefaction to come. Henry makes the sign of the Hippocratic Oath over the boy's sallow body, the swish of an S followed by a vertical slash through the same, and the boy's waxy features distort to demonic proportions. Knobby ram horns emerge from his scalp as horrible black fangs grow in stalactite clusters. For the finishing touch, a column of green vomit laced with economic shortcomings jets out of his mouth, *just* missing Henry.

"Now *that* was a close call," a feeble bon mot uttered for the benefit of no one besides Henry, instantly relegated to anemic irony when the sick boy breaks his bonds and lunges for the soft, pink meat under Henry's dimpled chin, an exquisite pocket of baby fat so succulent and juicy with generational privilege that a taste, and *just* a taste, cures the boy's manifold ailments.

Gibbering hysterically, Henry snatches a bone saw and stabs it in the boy's eye. Curtains of blood unravel from the cleaved socket and shroud the world in crimson despair. What have we done? What could we have done differently? The moment of reflection passes into insect memory. Intimate, undreaming pockets of what-could-have-been walled inside honeycombs scream for release, the watery cries muffled by the clamor of charlatans chanting platitudes from unbending summits of hypocrisy, insisting we smile cordially at vampires darkening sun-streaked valleys with their foul presence.

Pious men in androgynous uniforms listen to the thunder yet hear nothing but the dark silence of the cold night. They pull the covers up over shiny blank skulls and sink into the somnambulation of emotional severance. To tamp down the temptation to act in the interests of anyone besides themselves and pathological monoliths, they masturbate furiously for a thousand years.

Once their plumbing dries up from habitual self-abuse, the drab zealots enlist old crones in fishnet stockings, leather corsets and wimples to spit anticoagulant on the festering sores of Llump plague victims. Pamphlets containing antiquated advice on social diseases and childbirth are disseminated to mutilated Llump girls in mud holes, while Llump boys in an adjacent hole hear sermons about the glories of reproduction and the evils of contraception. Leaving nothing to chance, the old crones sabotage condom manufactures, with a special emphasis on condoms shipped to the segregated ghettoes of Llump Town. The night after the Festival of Darkness, all of Llump Town springs a leak. The Llumpulation explodes. There's no room anywhere for anyone, for about a week, after which the newborn Llumps shrivel up, die. Their work done, or undone as the case may be, the old crones hop a chartered jet (first class seats only, maximum comfort for those who comfort the comfortless) headed for the next bastion of misguided souls stricken by plague. The sun dips its face in the shimmering skin of a polluted New Tetraminion river, pick one, any one, and sinks in the silvery broth like a spent skipping stone.

"And that concludes my testimony." In cross-examination, the Committee snores thunderously, accompanied by choruses of juicy slumbering flatulence. "Sublime point, gentlemen. I'll have my people contact your people. Good day." Henry makes a fast break for the exit but cannot penetrate the thicket of counselors coaching star witnesses with the meticulous precision of watchmakers. Every word and thought must be perfectly executed. Nothing, however microscopic, can be left to chance. Scripts are handed out, retrieved, and returned, every page ragged and limp with red ink and the savage impatience of perfectionism. Closed circuit monitors broadcast withering crying jags live from hearing rooms as reporters with bodacious, high-ticket-dental-work smiles fail to convey the vaporous dread and stifling disharmony of inquisitional pressure. The network brass pats itself on the back and gives itself a raise for sending out neutered personalities incapable of communicating that lives are being destroyed one question at a time by handkerchief bureaucrats with harsh scarlet lips and sweaty comb overs. Compassionate as a hurricane, they overturn rocks undisturbed for decades, and with cheap trick efficacy, bone orchard prizes emerge from underneath to drag shocked defendants straight from the relative comforts of the frying pan and into the witch hunt bonfires.

Soaking wet with indefensible contradictions, the defendants weakly fend off salvos of unlubricated probes aimed up their fundaments. "By hook or crook, we'll get to bottom of this!" screeches a prickly-puss DA with a large knobby strap-on, the words TRUTH AND LIBERTY FOR ALL carved on the long quivering shaft.

The jury box, a pinchbeck prop untouched by so much as a drizzle of objectivity, writhes with toothless invalids fingering each other's stinkpot jinees and assholes. During deliberations, they guzzle sunrise-yellow piss from gummy specimen jars and gnaw on soggy sandwiches. Real disgusting spectacle. Blank pink gums and bluish tongues labor to dissolve bread and meat like flies spitting up digestive fluids. First round of ballots delivers a guilty verdict, even though no one paid any attention to the testimony or reviewed the evidence. No need. They all have the amazing ability to spot a guilty person just like that.

Jailbait cockteasers, hot young things in tighter than tight cotton shorts and gobs of misapplied mommy lipstick, falsely accuse the jurors of molestation, and an outraged public fills the deliberation chamber with Prussian blue pumped straight from the "dog pound," institutional slang for the old folks' home where swaybacked nags and other glue factory escapees measure out their final days in nondairy creamer and saccharine tablets. Court stenographers in gasmasks enter the chamber to transcribe mangled screams of choking death into machines calibrated to spit out spools of extenuating pretexts.

The verdict is read, everyone is guilty.

The last man out of the courtroom, Henry, dims the lights on another day of justice, which, more than anything in the world, is best served cold...

35.
Termination

FINAL REPORT ON MCRE/BLACK GOO TASK FORCE:

OCTOBER 14, 222 A.S.

WHILE THERE IS LITTLE DOUBT THAT PROPRIETARY FOOD ADDITIVES WITH CHEMICAL PROPERTIES SIMILAR TO CONTROLLED SUBSTANCES, OPIATES IN PARTICULAR, HAVE CONTRIBUTED TO THE HYSTERIA SURROUNDING THE MCREING EPIDEMIC, THERE IS NO EVIDENCE OF A STRONG CAUSAL LINK BETWEEN THOSE INNOCUOUS CHEMICAL COMPOUNDS AND THE URGE TO CANNIBALIZE RECYCLED CALORIES OR THE ACUTE CONSUMPTION OF BLACK GOO (A.K.A. GRINGE, LLUMP, SNAKE OIL).

UNLESS THE DEPARTMENT CAN DEMONSTRATE THAT THE FORMER CREATES A *BIOLOGICAL* NEED FOR THE LATTER, ANY SUCH CASE BROUGHT AGAINST THE AMERICAN FOOD ADDITIVE MANUFACTURERS ASSN. WILL BE CHALKED UP AS A MATTER OF SELF-DESTRUCTIVE CHOICE AND SUBJECT TO SUMMARY DISMISSAL.

ALTHOUGH THE DEPARTMENT IS DEEPLY INDEBTED TO SPECIAL AGENT WILLIAM VINE (DECEASED) FOR HIS EXTENSIVE FIELDWORK AND SACRIFICE IN THE LINE OF DUTY, IT IS OUR SWORN DUTY AS

KEEPERS OF THE PEACE TO CLASSIFY ALL DATA COLLECTED VIA PSYCHOMETRIC IMPLANT AS X1-RESTRICTED AND REDACT ALL TRACES OF HIM FROM THE PUBLIC ORGAN OF RECORD.

FINALLY, IN REGARD TO THE DEEP COVER PROGRAM, THE BOARD RECOMMENDS THE IMMEDIATE WITHDRAWAL OF ALL AT-RISK AGENTS FROM THE FIELD (BEGINNING WITH "POLY NOMIAL" AND "ORION POLARIS"), AND THAT THE PROGRAM BE SHELVED PERMANENTLY PENDING A HEARING FOR PROBABLE *TERMINATION*.

- HENRY KARLSON, SYSTEM LIAISON

R.A. Roth came into the world kicking and screaming, covered in blood and mucus. After a period of profound confusion, that continues to this very day, he took a wild leap into the mouth of literary madness. The years melted like chocolate under a sunlamp before he gained traction in a variety of notable lit mags. And then out of the blue, this happened (if this should become a smash hit and the phrase "overnight success" worms its way into a review, sixteen years is not "overnight," even in the context of a barren cliché). His next project is so secret even he doesn't know what it is, but rest assured that it will be unique. He doesn't believe in resuscitating echoes.

The New Bizarro Author Series

Her Fingers by Tamara Romero
Kitten by G. Arthur Brown
Janitor of Planet Anilingus
    by Andrew Wayne Adams
House Hunter S.T. Cartledge

2013-2014
The Mondo Vixen Massacre by Jamie Grefe
The Cheat Code for God Mode by Andy De Fonseca
Babes in Gangland by Bix Skahill
8-bit Apocalypse by Amanda Billings
Grambo by Dustin Reade
There's No Happy Ending by Tiffany Scandal
The Church of TV as God by Daniel Vlasaty

2014-2015
SuperGhost by Scott Cole
Pax Titanus by Tom Lucas
Deep Blue by Brian Auspice

2015-2016
King Space Void by Anthony Trevino
Rainbows Suck by Madeleine Swann
Arachnophile by Betty Rocksteady
Benjamin by Pedro Proenca
Rock 'n' Roll Head Case by Lee Widener
Slasher Camp for Nerd Dorks by Christoph Paul
Elephant Vice by Chris Meekings
Pixiegate Madoka by Michael Sean Le Sueur
Towers by Karl Fischer

2016-2017
Guitar Wolf by Nicholaus Patnaude
Hate From the Sky by Sean M. Thompson
Aunt Post by John Wayne Comunale
Tetraminion by R.A. Roth